THE
SEVENTEENTH
SWAP

THE SEVENTEENTH SWAP

Eloise McGraw

Troll Associates

For Lynn
who told me what I was trying to say

Contents

THE
SEVENTEENTH
SWAP

1

Jimmy-Day

It was Wednesday, April 6, raining. Jimmy-day, Eric Greene reminded himself as he slammed his desk shut.

He found himself smiling as he wove his way through the noisy 3:30 stream of his contemporaries and out the big double doors of Iron Mountain Elementary School. He was beginning to like Wednesdays —and Mondays and Saturday mornings—just about as well as the days when he could do whatever he wanted to. He'd never have believed it.

The rain was the wet kind, not the sort you could just ignore for a five-block walk, unless you wanted to be pretty damp when you arrived. Eric pulled up the hood of his all-purpose-all-weather-all-seasons jacket and zipped the front of it over his ring binder and math book—with difficulty, since the jacket was two years old and strained to its limit just covering *him*. Unfortunately the hood gave him tunnel vision and prevented his spotting Angel Anthony before she spotted him.

"Eric! Hey, Eric, wait! I got something to show you!"

He had half-turned at the sound of his name and now couldn't pretend he hadn't heard her. Also, the green light ahead of him was changing to amber. Resignedly, he waited at the Lake Street corner for Angel to cover the half-block that separated them, pumping along in the short-legged, hard-breathing way that never seemed to get her anywhere. He wished for the umpteenth time that her route home didn't coincide with his—or that it was possible to get from the school to the central section of town some other way than straight down Rivershore—old Bottleneck Boulevard. It wasn't, unless you cared to make a seven-mile detour around the lake, through what Eric thought of as the Rich-and-Fancy residential district. As for what Angel had to show him, it was bound to be either an A on her Language Arts theme or a new cocktail pick for her collection. He'd long ago used up his vocabulary of reactions to either one.

"Look! Isn't this *great?* My Aunt Julie brought it to me from *New York.* A *hotel* in *New York!*" Angel arrived at last, struggling to extract her hand from her jacket pocket, dropping a book as she did so.

Cocktail pick. Eric retrieved the book, shook the water off it and gave it to her, accepting in exchange a small black plastic sword with a gilded plastic hand guard, at which he gazed fixedly as he tried to think of something new to say. He failed. "Wow, another sword," he said as enthusiastically as possible. "How many does that make now?"

"Fourteen. Well, this one isn't really a *sword.*" The light changed and they started across the street. "It's more like a *cutlass.* See? It's curved. Like that kind pirates used to carry. It's the only one I have like that. Here, give it to me and I'll put it back in my box. Can you hold my books a minute?"

Eric balanced her books on his palm like a waiter with a tray while she located a small, flat tin box in one of her pockets, carefully opened its hinged lid, and put the cocktail pick inside. The box had printing on it. "Hey, lemme see that box a minute," Eric said. "Is that a cigar box? Hey, where'd you get it?"

Angel wasn't interested in letting him see it. "I don't know. Grampa's, I think." She snapped the box shut. "Did you have your picture taken today?"

Eric had not; but since everybody else in sixth grade had, he didn't bother to answer, allowing Angel to assume what she liked. He was still trying to read the printing. "Listen, if I found you another box, could I have that one?" he asked her.

"No, I need it for my cocktail picks." Angel stuffed the box into her pocket and took back her books.

"But I know somebody who collects cigar boxes. His name is Mr. Lee—he's the shoe repair man, down on—"

"Hey, Eric, how many pictures you going to order?"

Eric sighed. He never won conversations with Angel. "None. Who wants to spend money on dumb pictures?" Especially when there wasn't any money to spend.

"I'm going to order six wallet-sized ones, and one of the big ones to give my mom for her birthday."

They had cut over to Market Street; only three more blocks now. Angel chattered on happily, about her mother, her cocktail picks, her aunt from New York, her aunt from Idaho, her sister, her sister's best friend, the sister's best friend's boyfriend . . . Having no idea that bits of this monologue might later prove of crucial importance, Eric tuned her out, as he had learned long ago to tune out the succession of talkative women who had raised him—Aunt Myra in the dim past, cousin Anna Beth for a while after that, then for years and years Mrs. Wade, who used to arrive in the morning already talking, and finally the various high school girls who came in after school and made straight for the phone. His father had freed him from the last of them on the glorious day he turned nine. It had been blessedly silent around their apartment during the two years since.

He was just getting onto an interesting train of his own thoughts when Angel halted in the middle of the sidewalk and demanded impatiently, "Well, do you want to or not?"

Eric tried to play back her last few sentences as he glanced around for a clue. Oh, good. They were at Rose Lane, Angel's turnoff. "Want to?" he echoed cautiously.

"Want. To. Come. To. My house," Angel enunciated. "And see my sister's new *perfume* bottle. That her *friend* gave her. I've just been *telling* you."

"Oh. No. Thanks. I can't. I've got a job on Wednesdays."

"A *job?* Really?" Angel's attention was actually diverted from her own affairs for an instant. "What kind of job?"

"Sitter. Regular—three times a week. 'Bye, I

better go." Eric hastily turned his tunnel vision toward home and started walking at his own pace, which covered a lot more ground than Angel's.

"Whereabouts?" Angel called after him, but he pretended not to hear. If he told her she might decide to come talk to him there.

She gave up and went her way, down one of the last of the old streets still lined with small single houses and big trees, and with an increasingly light step he went his, into the oldest section of all—an area left over from the days when Iron Mountain was merely a little town grown up around an iron-rich hill which happened to be near a lake. The ironworks was long gone; the town's present focus was the lake and the boat slips and the water-skiing lives of people who had houses around its edges and jobs in the city eight miles away. The old houses Eric now walked past had nearly all been remodeled into offices or photo studios, or replaced long ago by apartments which were now dim and aging too.

His own apartment at the very end of Fifth Street was one of the dimmest, backed up against the old-growth timber edging the wooded ravine, and flanked by a patch of weeds which fell away into the steep brambly slope down to the railroad tracks. He had been walking faster and faster, wondering what Jimmy might want him to do this afternoon—something surprising, he was sure of that. By the time he reached the building he was loping, and he took the cracked cement steps three at a time, humming under his breath. He'd never have thought he'd feel this way about a job, especially this one. He'd have thought he'd hate having to stay cooped up indoors in one certain place for a certain length of time, having to be "company" for a little sick kid, having to give up his freedom, his treasured privacy, his treasured aloneness, which he'd spent a lot of his life achieving. Instead here he was looking forward to it.

There were things he had to do first—stop in the dingy little lobby to unlock mailbox 309, labeled "Greene" on a card worn almost to illegibility; collect the bills that were the only mail his dad ever got, and take them up two creaking flights of stairs with him; unlock the door of 309 to the familiar faint smell of damp towels and leftover coffee; dump his books and the mail, hang up his jacket, and walk through the living room into the kitchen to grab a couple of crackers and a glass of milk. After a detour via the back hall past both tiny bedrooms for a brief stop in the bathroom, he was free to leave again. With the apartment door dutifully locked behind him, he trotted back downstairs to the ground floor, followed the dim, musty-smelling hall to the extreme rear of the building and knocked on the door of 122, where the Nicholsons lived.

Jimmy's mother opened it at once—she had her coat on already, he noticed guiltily.

"It's all right, you're not late," she said as if she could read his mind. "I'm early. Couple of errands to squeeze in before work. Here he is, Jimmy! Bye-bye!" With a smile and a wink at Eric she hurried away down the hall.

Eric went on into the living room, where Jimmy was waiting in his wheelchair by the window, his thin little face already alive with eagerness to tell something, show something. Today it was an ad from last night's paper, of all things, the other pages of which lay scattered around him on the floor. Some kids' shoe store in the city was having a big close-out sale, starting today. *What do you care?* Eric almost said, but stopped himself in time.

"Here! Look at those cowboy boots!" Jimmy was exclaiming. "Wow! *Red* uppers, it says—with black designs on. And only seventeen ninety-nine, reduced from *twenty-five dollars*! Don't they usually cost lots more?"

"Yeah, I guess so," Eric said, though he didn't know much about it. He himself had never worn anything but tennis shoes from the chain store, one pair after another, differing only in their gradually increasing length. He studied the ad. "They must be made of something cheap. Yeah, all vinyl, it says."

"So what? They're a *steal*! I'd give my right eye for 'em," said Jimmy, who talked more like a man of thirty-odd than a boy of eight. His father, who was probably the only male he saw much of besides the doctor and Eric, *was* a man of thirty-odd.

"But what would you do without a right eye?" Eric teased idly. What he was thinking was: What would you do with the boots? Jimmy's legs, under the shabby afghan, were two pathetic little sticks that had never walked and never would. The warm socks he wore were the only footgear he'd ever need. Naturally Eric didn't say this, either. He changed the subject. "I found out how to make the airplanes."

"Honest? Already?" Jimmy's eyes, dark in his colorless little face, widened with delight. "Can you show me right now?"

"Yep. Can I use some of this newspaper?"

"Oh, sure. Help yourself. Only save my picture of the cowboy boots. I want to keep that."

"Hand me the scissors, then. I'll need them for the airplanes anyhow."

Jimmy passed the scissors and expertly spun his chair a little closer. "Let's make a lot, okay? All different sizes! Can I do one in my lap, or do you have to have a desk or something? How'd you find out how to do it?"

"I asked Willy Chung. He always knows stuff like that." Eric snipped his way around the shoe-store ad and held it up. "Where shall I put your picture?"

"Pin it up there on the window curtain where I can see it, okay?"

Eric obliged, feeling uncomfortable, even a little cross—not at Jimmy but at the shoe-store people for showing him one more thing he couldn't have. "Easy to make things look good in a picture," he told Jimmy carelessly. "At that price they'd probably wear out next week!"

Jimmy gave one of his sudden giggles. "Not if they were mine! They'd last forever if they were mine!"

Eric found nothing whatever to say to this, since it was true, but hardly a thing to giggle about—unless you were Jimmy, who seemed to regard his useless legs as some sort of bad joke that you either jeered at or ignored. Feeling rather shocked, and wishing he'd kept his mouth shut, Eric gathered the rest of the newspaper into a pile on the table and began on the first paper airplane.

"Is Willy Chung a friend of yours from school?" asked Jimmy, watching.

Eric caught a note of something—not quite envy, more like hunger—in Jimmy's voice, and didn't say, "My best friend," but merely nodded. There were a lot of things it would be mean to say to Jimmy— whether Jimmy giggled at them or not. Eric blundered into a few more every time he came. He'd always thought he and his dad were poorer than anybody; they didn't have a car or a color television or a bike— even a lousy fourth-hand bike—or any spare money, ever. But Jimmy didn't even have a best friend. He couldn't even go to school and meet anybody, not until he got strong enough so he wouldn't catch every single bug anybody else had. Last fall, when they'd tried to mainstream him in, he'd caught three colds and a strep throat right in a row, and ended up in the hospital. So now the home teacher came every morning and taught him here—which was okay in a way, Eric supposed, but home teachers didn't know the kinds of things kids learned from each other. Like how to make paper airplanes, or play poker, or tie a slip knot.

The fact was, Eric hadn't known many of those himself, until Jimmy'd started using him as a sort of Private Investigator in Charge of Finding Stuff Out. But if this kept up he was going to be the school expert on how-to-do-everything. He hoped he could remember how to make these paper airplanes. "Okay, now look, Jimmy, the first thing you do is fold your rectangle right across *here*. Like that. Then you take it and—"

"Wait—wait—lemme get some paper too!"

They made paper airplanes until they'd used up all the newspaper and had them sailing all over the room, landing on top of lampshades and each other's heads or under the bookcase or nose-down in Jimmy's empty orange-juice glass, and Jimmy was laughing so hard and getting so excited and so flushed over the cheekbones that Eric, who had his instructions from Jimmy's mother, thought it was time to call a halt. Besides, he was tired retrieving. He climbed on a chair to recover a last plane from the top of the window curtains, sailed it down into Jimmy's lap, and said, "Okay, let's ground 'em for refueling. How about refueling you? Want some more orange juice? Or you could have milk, if you're tired of juice."

Jimmy didn't answer. He was gazing past Eric's legs at the pinned-up picture on the curtains the way Eric might have gazed at the biggest chocolate sundae in the world.

Eric looked at his face a minute, feeling cornered. Then he jumped down and walked briskly out to the kitchen and poured two glasses of milk and opened cupboard doors until he found the plate of cookies, and carried the tray back to the living room. "Here you are. Drink up," he said.

Jimmy said, "Thanks," absently, reached for his milk, then focused. "Hey! How did you know there were cookies?"

"Smelled 'em when I came in the door," Eric confessed with a grin.

Jimmy grinned too. "I was supposed to tell you." Then, as usual, he darted up this diverting sidepath. "You could smell them? Honest? You've got a good nose! Mom made them early this morning. Could you tell they were chocolate chip?"

"I dunno." Eric tried to think back. "I don't think so. Your hall just smelled different. Maybe I just guessed it was cookies."

"How does our hall smell usually? No, tell me!" he insisted as Eric made waving, don't-ask-me motions. "I can't smell it at all because I'm here all the time. Does it smell like my medicine?"

The FBI could have used Jimmy. He was great at extracting information you didn't even know you had. Eric sighed, walked into the little entry hall, sniffed in a deep, concentrated breath and tried to analyze it. "Rubbing alcohol. Burnt toast. Something sort of sharp and lemony—"

"That's the dish detergent."

"And something else only I don't know how to say it. Something sort of brownish-purple."

"That's my medicine!" Jimmy exclaimed in triumph. "It must smell just like it tastes. What does *your* apartment smell like?"

Eric told him as well as he could. Mostly, he realized, it smelled of being closed up since breakfast and nobody being there—a lonesome smell. It made him feel sort of sorry for their apartment, which was a silly thought even for *him*.

"I'd like to collect smells," Jimmy announced.

"*Collect* them?"

"Sure. You could bring me some things to smell every Monday and Wednesday and Saturday, and Mom would bring me some others, and Dad could find things on his sales trips. Lots of people collect things, don't they? Even funny things, like old buttons. Mom told me."

"Oh. Well, yeah, they do. Willy Chung collects stamps. That's more usual, I guess. But I know a girl who collects cocktail picks—little plastic things they put in grown-ups' drinks," he explained before Jimmy could ask him what they were. "That's pretty funny. And Mr. Lee at the shoe-repair place collects cigar boxes." Then he wished he hadn't mentioned shoes, because Jimmy's eyes turned instantly to the picture of the cowboy boots.

"I'll bet those'd smell good," Jimmy said. "New leather! Like Dad's belt."

"New one hundred percent vinyl, you mean," Eric reminded him. "Like that lamp cord."

Jimmy only laughed as if he'd made a joke.

Eric began arranging the paper airplanes in rows on the table. "Anyway," he said idly, "your mom might buy 'em for you for your birthday."

Jimmy looked at him in astonishment, then laughed again. "Eighteen *dollars*? Then the doctor bill or gas bill or something wouldn't get paid again, and my dad'd want to know why, and they'd have another fight, and . . . oh, *you* know."

Eric didn't know. He didn't know anything about a life in which doctor bills arrived as regularly as gas bills, and your parents had fights. It occurred to him that there might be *some* advantages in a one-parent household. And many more in one where nobody was sick.

"What are you going to do, then?" he asked Jimmy. "About the boots?"

Jimmy shrugged blankly and said, "Nothing," as if it were obvious. Which of course it was.

2

The First Lists

Eric couldn't get it off his mind, though. By 5:45, when he climbed back upstairs to 309, a picture of those boots actually *on* Jimmy's feet had formed in his brain and lodged there, and wouldn't go away. Feeling all hollow and grumpy about it, he put the potatoes in to bake for dinner; by the time he shut the oven door he was wondering where he could get eighteen bucks.

Immediately the sum took on gigantic proportions. *Eighteen dollars?* Besides bus fare to get down to that shoe store and back? He seldom saw even eight dollars all at once, and when he did it was already earmarked for underwear or school supplies or something. Jimmy's folks ought to buy the boots. Could just $17.99 snarl up a whole month's budget?

He knew it could. Even $7.99 could—it depended on the budget. And the month. Look at Februarys and Septembers, when Dad had to send the child-support payments to Alice—the wife he'd divorced a long time before he married Eric's mother. Eric had never even seen Alice, or his half-sister Shirley—they lived clear across the country in Rhode Island. But he knew about them, all right. And he'd cheer as loud as anybody—in fact louder—when Shirley finally graduated from college, if she ever did, and he and Dad could stop paying half her bills.

Doctor bills—for somebody like Jimmy Nicholson —were probably even worse than child-support payments. And they came *every* month.

Okay. So neither Jimmy's mother nor his dad could buy Jimmy any dumb, useless cowboy boots. It was a silly idea anyway. So forget it, Eric ordered himself.

But Jimmy *wanted* them so much.

Eric wandered into the living room and dropped down into Dad's big chair in front of the little black-and-white TV, but he didn't turn it on, just sat there scowling at it, thinking, "But they're useless!" "But he wants them!" And all at once he understood. Jimmy wanted the boots because they *were* useless. Or rather, because his feet were. Such feet were no good at all for walking or running or even standing on. But at least they might look good. Look like real *feet*. Like cowboy feet—extra-fancy, extra-gaudy, bright red with black designs on. Wow.

At that point, Eric stopped fighting it, and started figuring.

His job paid fifty cents an hour plus all the cookies he could eat when there were any. About three bucks a week. It wasn't the best job he'd ever had but it was the best available at this time of year before lawns needed mowing or there was anything ripe to pick. You had to have a bike for practically anything else people'd hire a sixth-grader for—it was a fact of life he'd had to learn to live with. Besides, three bucks a week was all Jimmy's mother could afford. Trouble was, most of it had to go for notebook paper and stuff like that, because whenever he started earning, his allowance stopped. That had been his own idea. Dad hadn't said much—he never did—but he'd been surprised and grateful and proud of Eric, Eric could tell. There was no going back on the arrangement now. He could maybe save out a dollar a week. Big deal. The sale would be over and the boots on some other kid's feet long before he could save eighteen dollars that way.

So what else was there? How, Eric asked himself, did you get extra money when you needed a whole bunch, fast?

You sold something, came the answer as he glanced automatically toward the side wall where the big walnut bookcase used to stand. There were three narrow shelves there now, made of scrap lumber and cinder blocks, and a stack of leftover books on the table. There was a cheap digital clock on the table, too, instead of the big Seth Thomas that used to chime every fifteen minutes and bong the hour in a deep bass voice. It had been gone for years.

Eric got up and walked into his bedroom, wondering what he had to sell. His furniture was the kind made of pressed wood wherever it wouldn't show; the drawers stuck, the mattress and springs sagged in mismatched spots, and one leg of the desk was a chunk of dowel. He was used to it all and even fond of it, especially the desk, but probably nobody else would have it as a gift. Besides, it wasn't really his to sell—it belonged to Dad.

Except for his clothes and the checkers set and a few dilapidated little-kid books and toys, only three

things really belonged to him: his moss agate, his triangle stamp, and his mother's thimble. Eric worked
open the bottom desk drawer and got out the little
Chinesey box that held them. He supposed the box was
really his, too—Mrs. Wade had brought him some
peppermints in it one time and never asked for it back.
It was worn red lacquer on the outside, with a dimming
gold design in the middle of the lid and a small chip
off one lower edge. The inside was black lacquer, shiny
and good as new.

Eric took out the agate—he kept it wrapped in a
scrap of tissue paper so it wouldn't roll—and set it
aside. It was a good enough small agate, smoke-colored
with a clear pattern of black moss in its depths, but he
doubted if anybody would pay anything for it, or have
the least interest in it. To him it was a priceless treasure.
All he had to do was look at it and he was back on a
white beach on a sunny, blowy day long ago—after
his mother had died because he was maybe five years
old, but before Dad lost the library job—running
and running with a kite while Dad ran alongside
shouting encouragement. Later he'd built a huge sand
castle with a real moat around it and a handkerchief-
flag on top, still later devoured slightly sandy hot dogs
beside a driftwood fire, and finally walked slowly along
a graveled road to the old station wagon, staring hard
down into the gravel because Dad had said there were
sometimes agates mixed in. And he had *found* one—
this one. It was the totally magic end to a totally magic
day, the only vacation he and Dad had ever taken. The
station wagon had to be sold shortly after, when the
library job went; as Dad said, they didn't really need
a car.

He stuck his thumb into the box to take out the thimble—like Jack Horner pulling out the plum—and for a reluctant moment studied it. It really might be worth something—a few dollars anyway. Just above the wreath of little silver flowers around its edge, there were tiny flat squares that said "Sterling" and "Germany" when you looked at them through a magnifying glass. You could sell things made of sterling silver. The trouble was, this was the only thing he had left of his mother. Not that he remembered her; she had died before he was three years old. But sometimes—only sometimes—when he picked up this thimble, he suddenly saw thin, quick fingers and heard a certain delighted-sounding laugh. It hadn't happened when he picked it up today. He realized it happened very seldom now. Long ago—when the thimble came clear down to his knuckle, loose enough to twirl, instead of just perching on the end of his thumb like this—he could hear that laugh whenever he liked, just by staring at the silver flowers. He supposed he would soon quit hearing it at all. Then he supposed he could sell the thimble, and it wouldn't matter.

But—not yet.

There was still the triangle stamp. Eric looked at it and sighed. Willy Chung had been after him for that stamp for a year or more, ever since he first saw it. Willy collected triangle stamps—he had half a book full. Triangles from Liberia, from Monaco, from Hungary and Thailand, mostly with birds on; and one from someplace called Republik Maluku Selatan with a butterfly, which Eric thought the prettiest of all. But Willy had no stamp like Eric's. Eric's was sky-blue, and in the top point was the picture of a man in one of those Arab headcloths, and below him an oil well inside a sort of fat fleur-de-lis. At one side, in the blue part, were a couple of tents with a flag on a pole, and at the other three palm trees and a sand dune. Along one edge it said "Qatar Scouts" and "Postage," in English, and a big five, and just opposite there were squiggles that probably meant the same thing in Qatarese or whatever it was.

It was really interesting. And it was the only stamp Eric had—Willy had lots already.

"That's just the *point*," Willy always argued exasperatedly. "I *collect* 'em. I have a *reason* to want it. What good is it to you—just one dumb stamp?"

"If it's so dumb how come you're always after it?" Eric usually retorted, and that would be the end of it until the next time.

The fact was, he didn't have any better answer. He didn't know what good it was to him, or why he wouldn't give it even to Willy, who was his best friend. It was just *his*, that was all—and so few things were. Like the agate, it had come to him by chance—he'd found it wedged in the very back of a drawer the day Dad had brought his desk home from the second-hand shop, four years ago. It had seemed a dazzlingly good omen—not only was he getting a real desk of his own, he was getting a fascinating, mysterious little prize. The stamp had been his treasured possession ever since.

But now he wondered. It *was* a little silly to own just one stamp, when you were supposed to have whole books full. He'd never wanted any others; collecting things left him cold. But Willy wanted every triangle stamp he saw—he wanted every one in the world. He especially wanted Eric's, probably just because it was right there, under his nose, and yet not his. He was always offering to swap something for it. He'd even offered to buy it.

All right, Eric thought. I'll sell it to him.

But for how much? If it had cost five cents at the Qatar post office (or probably five some kind of Qatarese coins) what would it be worth now, in US money? You heard about people paying thousands of dollars for just one stamp—some rare one. They were nuts, in Eric's opinion, but live and let live. Anyhow, he doubted that his stamp was rare, or the least bit valuable to anybody but Willy. And while Willy's folks were comparatively well-off—he not only had a good bike but was campaigning for a twelve-speed to replace it—the price he could actually scrape together would fall a good bit short of even eighteen dollars. He probably had something under fifty cents in mind, judging from the items he'd offered to swap, at one time or another. For instance, his skin-tattooing ink—what was left of it after the two of them had spent a week drawing pictures on each other. His ballpoint pen that said "Souvenir of Indianapolis" and needed a filler. His Corgi auto collection—six trucks and a Jaguar—which he'd abandoned when he began on stamps.

Too bad Steve Morris didn't own the Qatar stamp, Eric reflected. Steve would have swapped in a minute for one of Willy's Corgi cars.

It was right about then that the light bulb went on in Eric's brain. It went off again a second later, leaving him with just a glimpse of a great idea. Of something that *might* be a great idea. It might equally well be a dud. But for that brief instant he'd peered down a long, intriguing vista of swaps and double-swaps and finagling, with a pair of red-and-black boots at the end. He was still staring hard at nothing, trying to make the vision come clearer, when he heard his dad's key in the lock.

By the time he'd put his possessions away and got to the entry hall, his dad was hooking his old red windbreak onto its nail and pulling on the even older turtleneck he always wore at home unless it was actually midsummer. He was a thin, middle-aged man and felt the cold.

"Hi," Eric said. "I put the potatoes in at quarter of six."

His dad smiled his slow, warm smile, gave him the usual penetrating glance, and nodded. It was at once a greeting, an acknowledgement of the potato report, and a gesture of satisfaction that Eric was there, was safe, that life was normal. He was a man of few words, but Eric was used to it.

Producing a butcher-wrapped package from the pocket of the red jacket, he held it up, announcing, "Steak!" and started for the kitchen, with Eric trailing him.

"Wow! Great!" Eric didn't have to ask the reason for the treat. His father worked at Mulvaney's supermarket, and sometimes got first crack at meat that had stayed overlong in the display case and was due to be marked down. It was always sort of purple instead of red, but there was nothing wrong with the taste. His dad got bargains in day-old bread, too, and lettuce past reviving, and vegetables going limp. Neither he nor Eric was fussy. Food was food.

"Jimmy doing okay?" he asked Eric as he unwrapped the package on the drainboard.

"Yeah. We made paper airplanes half the afternoon. He's decided to collect smells. I'm supposed to
think of smelly things to bring him."

Mr. Greene shook his head, chuckling. "Take him
some garlic."

"Hey, I will! Could you get a discard from Marvin?" Marvin was a former Iron Mountain High School
linebacker, now produce manager at Mulvaney's—to
Eric's intense but private disapproval. In his opinion
Dad should have had the job, and *could* have, if he'd
just pushed himself forward a little at the right moment.
But that was two-year-old water under the bridge. As
his dad nodded, he went on with the news bulletins. "I
got a B on the Social Studies test. That's a *little* better
anyhow. We didn't have the math one—they took the
school pictures today." Then he was sorry he'd mentioned that, because the amusement faded from his
dad's face, leaving it tired and impassive again, not
even pleased about the steaks. He was always that way
when Eric automatically passed up something they
couldn't afford. Eric said quickly, "I was glad *I* got
out of *that*. I wouldn't give you a dime for any dumb
pictures of me. They always turn out lousy."

"I'd've kinda liked one," said his dad unexpectedly.
Before Eric could do more than stare—because why
would he want one when he saw Eric every day?—
he added, "Time to make the salad," and the subject
was closed.

Eric took the lettuce out of the refrigerator and
got busy. That was enough jabbering for tonight anyway. Dad had probably said that to make him feel
somebody would want his pictures. But *he* didn't, and
he wished Dad would believe it. In fact of all the

things Dad's salary wouldn't run to, he probably cared least about those pictures. He hadn't got around to mentioning Jimmy's cowboy boots, and he now realized he wasn't going to—at least not yet. But as he worked with the salad and later as he sat opposite his dad chewing steak, his mind kept going back to his maybe-great idea, trying to see it clearly, trying to pin it down.

It had to do with Steve Morris wanting something Willy had, but having nothing to swap that Willy wanted—and with Eric being middle-man. That much he knew. And he could plainly see that Willy and Steve would be delighted with the transaction. But where would it leave *him*? That's what he couldn't figure. How could it get him any closer to those boots?

He squinted his eyes and concentrated. Suppose he swapped the stamp to Willy for the Corgi cars, and swapped the cars to Steve for something else. Then, if he could find somebody who wanted the something else . . . He could see right now he was going to have to do a little research.

After dinner, he phoned Steve Morris and asked him what he'd give for any one of six Corgi trucks, or a Jaguar.

"Wow! You mean that kind of Jaguar Willy Chung has? Have *you* got one?"

"I think I can get one," Eric said cautiously. "How much would you—"

"Are any of the trucks those milk trucks? Or a moving van? I been looking all over for a moving van."

"I don't know. I'll find out. If one of 'em was, how much would you—"

"Only place around here that sells Corgi cars is the variety store, and they don't keep enough in stock.

I've already got everything they have! And I can't get Mom to take me down to Tony's Toytown because she says . . ."

With difficulty, Eric got him back to the point.

"Oh. Well, I already spent my allowance. I could swap you a box kite, though. It's only got one little tear in it. Or my thunderegg rock. Or a Swiss Army knife with two blades and a screwdriver and bottle opener. One of the blades is broke, but . . . Oh yeah, or I could let you have a T-shirt with Mount St. Helens on it. It says 'I survived.' Only washed a couple times. I outgrew it."

Eric absorbed this information in doubtful silence.

"Well? Is it a deal?" Steve asked him anxiously.

"I'll let you know." Eric hung up, found a pencil and his ring binder, turned it upside down and wrote on the back page:

THINGS PEOPLE WILL SWAP

1. *Triangle stamp*
2. *Corgi cars*
3. *S. A. knife (one blade broke)*
4. *Thunderegg rock*
5. *Box kite (small tear)*
6. *Mt. St. H. T-shirt, good cond.*

He studied his list, then on the opposite side of the page wrote:

THINGS PEOPLE WANT

1. *Triangle stamp*
2. *Corgi cars (esp. Jag. & Mov. van)*

After some thought, he added to the second list:

3. *Cocktail picks*
4. *Cigar boxes*
5. *Smells (?)*

That last one didn't really count. What else? He dimly remembered Angel yakking on and on about somebody being crazy about little china dogs. But was it her sister or her aunt from New York, or her sister's friend's boyfriend, or . . . *Now* he wished he'd listened. He'd better let her catch him tomorrow, and see if she'd say it all again. Meanwhile . . .

"Homework done already?" Dad asked as he came in wearing his robe and slippers, and dropped into his TV-watching chair.

"Just about to start," Eric told him, and turned his ring binder right side up.

He'd already made a start, of sorts, on what he was beginning to think of as The Great Double Multiple Swap. Tomorrow he'd better get busy with that research.

3

Research

Eric learned a lot the next day about finding out what you want to know without quite knowing what it is you want to find out.

He filled all the cracks of the forenoon with asking questions of people—sometimes direct ones, like "If you could have anything you wanted for under a dollar, what would it be?", sometimes leading ones like "Would you rather have a Swiss Army knife with one blade broken instead of your little one?"

By lunchtime he was just making random remarks to see what came of them, and discovering that a great deal did. "Chris Donaldson's grandpa's got about a hundred old license plates nailed up in his garage," he told Melinda Jones, who retorted, "That's nothing, *my* grandpa's got *his* garage full of old radios he's rebuilding—he has to keep his car in the street." Later when he happened to mention to Ms. Larkin, the school librarian, that his dad's old copy of the *Just-So Stories* didn't have colored pictures like the library's, she exclaimed, "I'll bet his has Kipling's own black-and-white drawings! Oh, what I'd give for a good copy of that edition!"

By the time Eric started home from school he'd added several items to both his lists and was counting on Angel to add some more. It was a letdown to spot her trotting off in the opposite direction, jabbering ninety-to-nothing at Debbie Clark as they both headed for Debbie's mother's car and, presumably, Debbie's fancy house down beside the lake. After a little thought, Eric changed his own direction, crossed at the light, and started up Lake Street toward the stores. At least it wasn't raining, though the day was overcast and chilly.

A couple of blocks along, nearly opposite Mulvaney's Supermarket where Eric's dad worked, was Mr. Lee's little hole-in-the-wall business, squeezed between a copy shop and a sandwich bar like a thin burger in a bun. Eric peeked through the space separating the big "E" of "SHOE" from the "R" of "REPAIR" lettered on the smudgy display window and saw that no customers were waiting in the narrow space in front of the counter. The bell jingled as he pulled open the door, producing a brief shout of acknowledgement from the depths of the shop, unintelligible over the whine of one of the machines.

"It's only me, don't hurry," Eric shouted back. He leaned his elbows on the scarred wooden counter, smoothed over and dark with multiple coats of varnish. Waiting for the whine to give way to the flapping sound that meant the machine was idling, he shut his eyes and drew a deep, analytical breath of the pungent atmosphere. Leather, of course—new and old. Machine oil. Shoe polish. A hint of French fries, probably left over from Mr. Lee's lunch, always sent in from Shari's

Sandwich Express next door by his wife, who was Shari. And something like glue—maybe all those plastic sacks encasing arch supports and things, hanging from the pegboard at his elbow. Anyway, lots of smells for Jimmy.

"Well, if it isn't my pal Eric," said Mr. Lee, coming around the half-wall from the rear of the shop, leaving the machine panting like a big, noisy dog with its tongue lolling out and its tail thumping. He was a short, wiry man with big hands and black curly hair going a little thin in front. "What'll it be, more shoelaces already?"

"No, I was just wanting to ask you something—about your cigar boxes that you showed me once. Did you ever have any *tin* ones? Or do you only like the wood kind?"

"Tin ones?" Mr. Lee's dark eyes got the little spark in them that meant he was interested. "You don't mean Between the Acts? Little flat hinged box, gold-colored, about so square, with six holes in a circle in the bottom, red lid with black lettering, light blue revenue stamp?"

"I'm not sure about the holes," said Eric, trying to visualize Angel's box. "I only saw it for a minute, and it was full of cocktail picks."

"Full of *cocktail picks?*" echoed Mr. Lee with a bark of laughter.

Eric explained Angel's use of the box. "She said she found it at her Grandpa's."

"I'll bet she did. In the attic at that. Those boxes went out just about the time I was cutting my teeth. Second World War stuff. What d'you think she'd take for it? Now, don't say cocktail picks." Mr. Lee held up a palm. "I'm not a drinking man and if I was I wouldn't set foot inside any rip-off cocktail bar."

"Would you pay money for that kind of box?" asked Eric, holding his breath.

Mr. Lee thought about that a minute. "Would she take a dollar-fifty?" he asked Eric.

Eric's expectations deflated. "I don't know."

"They're not worth more'n two bucks according to the list books—trouble is, I never yet come across one to buy. Tell you what—I'll give her better'n that in work. She need any shoes reheeled?"

"I guess not. She always wears tennis shoes, same as me." Eric sighed. "She might not want to give that box up anyway. I tried to get it for you yesterday and she wouldn't listen."

The little spark came back into Mr. Lee's eyes and became a fanatical little light. He drummed on the counter with his stubby, work-grained fingers. "Listen, Eric. Talk to her, will you? Sound her out. I won't deny I'd like to have that box."

"*She* usually does the talking," said Eric doubtfully. "But I'll try." He turned to go, then whirled back. "Oh, I nearly forgot. Mr. Lee, have you got any little scrap of new leather you'd give me? Or an old shoe-polishing rag?"

"An old—?" Mr. Lee chuckled and muttered, "What next, boy?" but after a moment's thought he headed for his workbench behind the partition. He came back with a thick curl of shoe-sole like the trimming from a giant fingernail, and an aromatic dirty rag. "There you are—you can have 'em if you'll tell me what you want with 'em."

"I've got a friend who collects smells," Eric explained, and left the shop with Mr. Lee's crack of laughter following him.

He was getting hungry. A stop at Mulvaney's might fix that, besides producing more information. He crossed the street at the corner by the bike store, slowing as he passed to run a connoisseur's eye over the window-ful of shiny new Schwinns and racers, then walked into the covered shopping mall and through the big auto-matic sliding doors of the supermarket at its far end. His dad was filling in at Number Three checkstand, as he often did during the periodic little rushes when the handful of shoppers unhurriedly wandering the store simultaneously completed their purchases and became an impatient crowd lined up with loaded baskets. There was only one customer left at Number Three. As Mr. Greene waited for the computer-register to calculate the charges, he spotted Eric and raised a beckoning finger.

Eric hung around the Daily Special display—canned smoked oysters, *yuck*—until the customer de-parted with the box boy at her heels, and his dad turned off the Number Three light and joined him. Reaching into the pocket of his green cotton jacket, he produced a Canadian dime and a buffalo nickel, which he flipped to Eric with a smile.

Whenever Dad worked the checkstand he kept an eye out for oddball coins, replaced them in the cash register with ordinary ones of his own, and brought the funny ones home to Eric, who took them to Mrs. Panek next time he thought of it. Mrs. Panek's brother was a disabled veteran of the Korean war, who lived with her in the cramped rooms back of the little newspaper-magazine-card-and-candy shop created from one of the old houses on Heron Street just up from the post office. He collected coins.

"Maybe I'll walk up to the Paneks' now. Only—is it okay if I dump my books here while I'm gone?" Eric asked his father.

"If Marvin says so."

Marvin wouldn't mind. Giving a heave to his bulging ring binder and three outside reading library books, which were becoming a real drag to cart around, Eric headed through the bins and fruity pyramids of the produce department to the swinging doors at the rear of the store. Beyond them, in a cement-floored area stacked with boxes and untidy with vegetable trimmings, Marvin was unloading crated lettuces from a truck backed up to the open bay, and exchanging jocular insults with the driver. They had to yell over the throttled-down blare of rock music coming from the little radio on a shelf. Eric set his books down in a safe corner, unkinked his shoulders with relief, and glanced, he hoped not too obviously, toward the broad wooden counters flanking the sink, where discards were set aside.

"Them Golden Delicious got to be throwed out," Marvin called helpfully, swinging a final crate to the floor and waving all-clear to the driver. As the truck's motor roared, he sent the big door rattling along its rails and came toward Eric, wiping his hands on his apron front. He still looked more like a high school linebacker than a department manager, to Eric's preju-diced eye, but the bitter resentment he'd felt at first on his dad's account had given way to a grudging admission of Marvin's competence, and finally to a reluctant liking. You just couldn't stay mad at some-

body as big as a moose and friendly as a cocker spaniel.
"Go ahead," he was urging Eric now, pushing one of
the big knives toward him. "Take a couple apples—
just trim them bruises off. Want a limp carrot?" He
was already scrubbing one under the tap. "How's school
going? Learn any new jaw-breaker words today?"

" 'Metaphorically' and 'lackadaisical'," Eric re-
ported, slicing off the crushed end and biting into his
first apple. He pulled his Language Arts word list out
of his ring binder and handed it over in exchange for
the carrot.

"Wow*ee*!" Marvin exclaimed, holding it gingerly
in wet hands and shaking his head over it. "How about
that 'reprehensible'! What's that mean?"

Eric only grinned and ate his apple. Marvin had
great dramatic gifts. His speech might sound like the
locker room, but Eric happened to know he'd gradu-
ated from Iron Mountain High with honors.

"Marvin," he said when he'd returned the list to
his notebook and started on his carrot. "Do you know
anybody who collects rocks? Good ones, I mean. Like
thundereggs."

"A rock hound, hm? No, I guess not. I know somebody collects campaign buttons—that do you any
good?"

"What're they?"

"You know—them big round things you pin on
your lapel that say 'Joe Blow for Mayor.' Stuff like
that. They're all over the place in election years. Old
Jake, in the meat department, he's got 'em clean back
to the first Roosevelt campaign. Must have hunnerds."

"You mean Mr. Forrester?" Eric said in some awe.
He had never heard the formidable head butcher re-

ferred to in any less respectful terms. "D'you think he'd pay money for one, if I could find a good one?"

"Depends how good it is—and whether he's already got one like it. I'll tell you one thing, though." Marvin started wrenching lettuce crates open. "People'll pay money for just about anything—so long as they want it bad enough."

He heaved an opened crate onto a shopping basket, and whistling expertly along with the rock band, bumped the swinging doors open and went through. Eric followed, waved goodbye to him at the lettuce bin, and started out of the store. He was intercepted once more by his father, now stamping prices on canned goods at the top of Aisle D.

"Might as well get my newspaper while you're at it," he told Eric, digging a handful of coins from his pocket and selecting a quarter. Then with a closer look, he picked out a penny, too. "Must've come by this one honest," he said with a grin as he handed both coins to Eric.

"Wow, thanks!" Eric said, and went on his way, studying the penny. It was the kind with wheat on the reverse—Mrs. Panek's brother liked those. He'd probably like the nickel and the Canadian dime, too. He liked nearly anything. "It gives him something to do," Mrs. Panek always explained sorrowfully.

Until today, Eric had always just swapped Dad's funny coins to her for other ordinary ones, sometimes receiving a candy bar as a bonus.

Today, for the first time, it occurred to him that a wheat-sheaf penny might be worth more than just one cent. Lots, lots more. Coins were like stamps—the rare ones brought big prices. The wheat-sheaf ones hadn't been made since the early 1940s, Dad had said so. After that they'd made them out of zinc—for just one year, 1942 or '43, Eric could never remember which —but it was Dad's birth year. He always said he was born in the year of the zinc penny.

Eric wondered suddenly—with a sinking feeling— if he'd ever handed over a *zinc* penny to Mrs. Panek for just one cent. Mrs. Panek wouldn't have noticed—she knew no more about coins than he did, mainly that some were odd and most were not. But her brother would know, all right. The zinc ones *must* be scarce if they'd made so few of them. Just one might be worth the whole price of the boots.

The very thought made him hurry, though he had no idea what he'd do about it if he *had* let go of a fortune without realizing it. Maybe Frank—that was Mrs. Panek's brother—would at least give the penny back to him, so he could take it to a coin shop to sell. But maybe Frank had sold it himself by now. Maybe for twenty or thirty dollars. Maybe . . .

He had got about that far when he ran up the four rebuilt steps and past the newspaper-vending rack to the door. It wasn't like any other door he went through regularly, being carved and ornamented under its layers of smart blue paint, and set with a pane of glass etched with the picture of a deer in a forest. Mrs. Panek was behind the counter, bent over to get out a pack of cigarettes for her customer, a man in a gray running suit. When she straightened up, she was half a head taller than he was.

"You shouldn't, really," she told him sorrowfully— she nearly always sounded sorrowful about things. "They're so bad for you."

The man gave her a faintly startled look, muttered, "Yeah, I'm gonna quit one of these days," and jogged out of the shop and away, pocketing his cigarettes.

"Now, I hope he means that," Mrs. Panek said with a sigh. "Eric, honey, what'll it be for you today?"

Eric dug in his pocket for the Canadian dime, the buffalo nickel, and the wheat-sheaf penny. "I brought your brother some coins, and—and I—wanted to ask him a question."

"Why, sure. Lemme see if he's waked up from his nap yet. He hasn't been too perky, last few days, I dunno what it is; this weather, maybe . . ."

As she spoke, she edged through the curtained doorway behind her, her hips nearly touching at both sides. She was shaped exactly like a mammoth pear on legs. Eric waited, staring around the familiar little shop with its revolving card rack, its opened cartons of candy bars in the glass case, its stack of *Wall Street Journals* on the counter weighted with an old metal thing that looked like an iron without a handle. He was already feeling ashamed of himself for even imagining that Frank might have cheated him. He'd probably never even brought a zinc penny in here, and if he had—

"He's awake," said Mrs. Panek, reappearing. "You go right on back, honey, and take him your coins. Watch out for the mousetraps—I got 'em all over the place. Pesky things steal my bait if I use cheese, and won't touch it when it's bacon. Frank says I'd ought to get a cat, but I don't know, some cats are lazy, and the toms, they prowl . . ."

Leaving her to argue it out with herself, Eric slipped past the end of the counter and between the drooping, dusty-smelling curtains, and walked down the narrow passage to the sitting room at the back, which always reminded him of a sort of cozy, over-stuffed nest. Mrs. Panek had moved Frank here when her husband died, trading her walnut orchard for this house and business, leaving behind ten rooms, a barn, and fifty years of memories, but almost none of her possessions. Consequently this room was full of every-thing—two or three of everything. Every surface was crowded with objects, every wall with pictures, and there were several little rugs on top of the big one.

Frank sat hunched in his usual armchair, with one of his coin books open across his knees. He was a big, gaunt man with skeletal hands, but his eyes were lively. He peered up at Eric from under his eyebrows—his back wouldn't straighten, hadn't for thirty-two years—and smiled a greeting.

"Set down, set down. Sis says you got me another good penny," he said in his funny wavery voice.

"Couple of other things too." Eric handed him the coins, sat on the end of the sofa where there weren't any little pillows, and watched him as he held his magnifying glass over the penny, murmuring, "Good. Nineteen forty. I need that," and nodded in a satisfied way over the others.

Eric cleared his throat. "That book you've got there—does that tell you stuff about what coins are worth? I mean certain ones?"

"That's what it does. You got something you want looked up?"

"Oh—I just wondered. Like, well, those wheat pennies. What're they worth?"

"Not much." Frank flipped pages, ran a bony finger

down the columns, found an entry. "If you got a hun'erd of 'em, they'll fetch you a dollar ten."

"Oh," said Eric. That really *wasn't* much. Of course those weren't a bit rare. Now for the real question. "How about zinc pennies? The ones they only made back in—"

"I know. I know. Now, those'll be a good bit more." The finger found another entry. "Here y'are. Zinc pennies. Ten cents apiece."

"Ten *cents?*" Eric's faith in a possible coin bonanza collapsed into rubble.

"That's a thousand percent increase," Frank pointed out. " 'Course, if I had one, I wouldn't sell it."

"If I ever find one, you can have it," Eric told him, getting up to go. He had abruptly lost interest in coins.

"Keep a watch for the Indian Heads. That's my specialty," Frank said. "Thanks for these others, kid. You tell Sis to slip you a candy bar on the way out."

"Oh, that's okay. So long." Eric pushed back through the curtains, glancing at the big clock over the cigar counter. Might as well go on home and stare at his lists as to keep on tramping around like this, accomplishing nothing. He was beginning to feel a strong need of advice, without the dimmest notion of where to go for it, or precisely what to ask for when he got there.

Mrs. Panek was standing below the high west window, stretched like the Statue of Liberty to reach the eyelet in the blind. It had lost its regular cord and she used some kind of little handled hook to pull it down. "Looks like the sun's gonna come out just in time to set," she remarked as she captured the blind and adjusted it. "And weatherman says more rain tomorrow." She sighed and walked heavily back behind the counter. "Well, that's April for you. Here, don't forget your sixteen cents."

Eric pocketed the substitute coins, paused outside the door to buy his dad's newspaper from the vending rack, and walked back to Mulvaney's to retrieve his schoolbooks. Heavy-laden, and wishing for the millionth time he had a bike of some sort—any sort—he plodded back across Lake Street and on down Cedar past the bakery and Jill's Fabric Shop where Jimmy's mother worked, and the ski-shop and Harry's Hair Parlor and the whole block of the new savings and loan building and another block of leftover old houses straggling toward the ravine, finally turning down Fifth Street toward home.

He hadn't chanced to walk this way in a week or two. It was when he was crossing Governor Street that a familiar huge maple caught his eye up ahead, towering over a ramshackle old vacant house now stranded between the new insurance building on the corner and the vet's clinic on beyond. Cholly! Eric suddenly knew where he might try for advice.

He followed the down-sloping path around the side of the house, which backed on the ravine, and found Cholly standing in the open basement doorway, a short, square, shaggy old man peering closely at the handle of a battered saucepan, where a patch of new solder caught the graying afternoon light.

"That should hold," Cholly remarked with a bob of his head that made his forelock dip and spring up again. He never said hello when somebody joined him, just went on aloud with whatever conversation had been going on in his head. "Old Missus Fawdiss, she thinks the world an' all 'o this pawt. Won't have nought t'do with the modren ones. Can't say's I blame her, lot of 'em's trash. Come on inside. Still turns kinda nippy this tima day."

Charlie Merton—known to Eric as Cholly Mutton because that was how Cholly pronounced his name—had emigrated from Plymouth, England in some unimaginable long ago past, and since then, to judge from his rambling stories, had lived in every one of the fifty states. When Eric had first encountered him a couple of years back he had just taken up residence in this basement. Until somebody bought the house to remodel into something, Cholly lived in the lower regions rent-free in exchange for seeing that nobody actually burned it down. Fortunately, the sloping lot allowed some daylight to seep through one extremely dirty window. Cholly's tastes were not fussy, and he made do quite comfortably with a few sticks of furniture the last tenants had abandoned, plus his own pack-rat huddle of possessions. And as he had told Eric unanswerably, the price was right.

Eric followed him down the two crumbling cement steps into the dim little room he had created in the area nearest the window by ranging his bits of furniture in a sort of semi-circular fence, beyond which the cavernous reaches of the basement vanished into shadow, with only the looming shape of the furnace visible in the gloom. Dropping his books on the rock-hard old daybed and himself beside them, Eric wondered how much he should explain to Cholly about the boots, and why Jimmy wanted them so much, and why he himself had got so pig-headedly determined that Jimmy would have them. He wasn't entirely sure he *could* explain it so anybody'd understand.

Meanwhile, Cholly was tidying his cluttered worktable, clearing away solder and soldering iron, rattling noisy bits of screws and things into the old coffee cans lined up on the shelf, and still rambling on about Mrs. Fordyce's pot. " 'Missus, that pawt's an antique,' I told her. 'You could sell that thing for money!' but she won't hear of it, she's used to it and it's used to her. She's an antique herself, ahter all." Cholly sat down on his carpet-covered piano stool in front of the worktable, clutched both knees with his gnarly hands, and grinned through his whiskers at Eric. "Wouldn't doubt she's older'n *I* am. And that's older'n God."

"I thought antiques were fancy chairs and tables, and chinaware and things—not old mended pans," Eric said.

"Depends on your pocketbook, son—and the year you was born. Why, this basement here, it's fulla antiques, way they think of 'em now. You take a look sometime in that Hobbyhorse Shop. 'Bout halfway down Long Alley, there behind the p'lice station. Tell Maggie Teggly you're a friend of mine—I've done odd jobs for her, she'll let you gawp around. Take my word, I've seen things in there with fancy price tags that were give away with movie tickets when I was young."

"*Given* away? With *movie tickets?*" Eric echoed.

"That's right! Used to be, a chap and his gal could collect a whole set of dishes just doin' their courting at the picture show. Hard to believe nowadays. Why, Maggie's got old pawts like this one in that shop! Old potato-smashers like the one I use meself. Old *telephones*, the kind with a crank, used to hang on the wall. Old pop bottles! Old photos of nekked babies lying on their stomachs! You name it, Maggie Teggly's got it—and she sells 'em, too."

Vivid pictures of Mrs. Panek's sitting room were dancing in Eric's mind. "Where does Maggie Teggly get all that stuff in the first place, Cholly?"

Cholly shrugged, leaned back with his elbows propped on the worktable. "Folks bring 'em in, let 'er sell 'em on commission. I've even known her offer to buy. See this here little tool-carrier I keep my screw-drivers in?" He half-turned, lifted a small wooden tray by the fingerholes in its central divider. "She's been ahter me to name my price for that ever since I carried it to her place once to put up some shelves. But I said, "No, Ma'am." My pa made that for hisself before we ever come to this country. It'll be mine until I die. Care for a cuppa, son? I'm about to put me *antique* kettle on."

"I'd like to—but I've got to get home," Eric told him, hurriedly gathering up his books after a glance at Cholly's battered clock. "Maybe Saturday, if you're here?"

"Any time, no need for no engraved invitation. See you around, then."

"See you, Cholly. And thanks!" Eric called back as he stepped outside. Cholly might not know it, but he'd given his usual valuable advice without hearing even a word about the boots.

4

The Hobbyhorse Shop

After his homework was done that night Eric turned his ring binder upside down so that the first page was the back page, and studied his lists again.

They looked shorter than he remembered, even with the few items he had added so confidently at school, when he was just getting started on his research. Those were probably worthless. He somehow felt much less sanguine now about finding old license plates for Chris Donaldson's grandpa, or old radios and records for Melinda Jones's. He had no idea where one might come across such things. Reluctant but realistic, he drew a line through both items.

There remained that note he had scrawled about Ms. Larkin wishing she had a *Just-So Stories* like Dad's. He liked Ms. Larkin. She was such an enthusiastic sort of lady, and always had time to answer your questions. He'd often thought of mentioning to her that his dad used to be a librarian, too. But he'd never done it. She'd be bound to ask where Dad worked now, and what had happened, and how he could give up library work after all that training, and a lot of other questions of whose answers Eric had never been quite sure.

Anyway he'd like her to have the kind of *Just-So Stories* she wanted. The question was, would Dad want to give his up? Eric wasn't sure he should even ask. Dad had owned that book since he was a little kid—somebody had written "Happy Eighth Birthday to Mitchie" in the front. He'd hung onto it all these years. On the other hand, he never read it now, and Eric could plainly hear Ms. Larkin saying, "Oh, what I'd give for a good copy of that edition!" What if she'd give five dollars? Even ten?

Eric jumped up from his desk, went into the living room to the makeshift bookshelves, and found the old gray book with its raveled, familiar spine, which he had helped wear out. Hesitantly he opened it and riffled through the pages, creating a little breeze on his face that smelled of ageing paper and memories. Then he stopped abruptly at the beginning of "The Elephant's Child", which had once started, like all the other stories, with a huge, fancy capital letter enclosed in a decorative square. Now it started with a hole—a slightly ragged squarish hole cut right out of the page long ago by Dad himself. There were holes in half the other beginning pages—how could he have forgotten that? Dad had sheepishly confessed—warning Eric *never* to mutilate books—that he'd used the fancy initials in some school assignment that had seemed terribly important at the time. He'd had to recall for Eric—or invent—the square of missing words on the other side of those pages, until Eric knew the stories so well he could do it for himself. Eric returned the volume to the shelf, secretly relieved. He and Dad could keep their favorite book. Ms. Larkin wanted a "good copy." This wasn't it.

Back to his desk, and the now even shorter lists. A careful review of his day did little to lengthen them, and less to match them up. He wished Marvin had been acquainted with a rock hound instead of a campaign-button collector—then somebody would want Steve's thunderegg. As it was, he could only add, under

THINGS PEOPLE WANT:

> *Old campaign buttons (Mr. Forrester in meat dept.)*
> *Indian Head pennies (Frank)*
> *Antique Junk (Hobbyhorse Shop)*

Under **THINGS PEOPLE WILL SWAP**, he wrote,

> *Reheeling job.*

Then, after a good deal of pencil nibbling and mental wandering around Mrs. Panek's sitting room, he added,

> *Antique junk?*

He stared at the lists with growing doubt. The final two items matched, but for all he knew, Mrs. Panek felt the same about her jumble of possessions as Missus Fawdiss did about her "pawt." Sighing, he erased the heading of the second list and changed the "WILL" to "MIGHT."

That seemed to be all he could do until he talked to Angel again, and had a look at that Hobbyhorse Shop, so he shut the ring binder and went to bed.

Leaping down the stairs next morning on his way to school, he saw Mr. Evans, the apartment manager,

just backing out of his first-floor doorway like some
large, round-shouldered turtle withdrawing from its
hole. And suddenly he realized that *he* knew a rock
hound himself. At least, he supposed Mr. Evans would
qualify, though the rocks Eric had occasionally seen—
and stumbled over—in his dim little living room
seemed more like what you'd find in a magpie's nest
than a real "collection." However. No harm in trying.
Eric stopped at the foot of the stairs to say hello.

Slowly, the way he did everything, Mr. Evans
turned himself about, taking several little shuffling steps
to get all the way around to face Eric, then nodded ami-
ably. "Howdy, howdy. Nite day," he mumbled. He
usually didn't wear his teeth except when you came to
pay the rent, though he always kept them handy in his
shirt pocket, for emergencies.

"Yeah, it is," Eric agreed with a glance toward the
two glass panels that flanked the front door. Sure
enough, the sun was shining, though he'd been too
preoccupied to notice. At the risk of being late to
school, he seized the moment. "Mr. Evans, I was wondering—would you be interested in a thunderegg for
your rock collection? Or have you already got one?"

"Hm? Mm. Shunderegg, eh? Mm. Gah a uncuh
one. Nah wursh mush lesher cuh. You gah one you
wanna geh riub?"

Translating this with some difficulty, Eric said,
"Not to get *rid* of, exactly. And it's not mine yet—but
I think I could get one from my friend, and it *is* a cut
one. With the cut part polished. It's real pretty, I've
seen it."

"Hm! Whasher pren wan borit? Prolly doo mush. I
gahno money shpare."

"Well—maybe I could work out a swap. That is, if you had something . . ."

"Gah other rocksh. 'Shbow all."

Other rocks. That was his problem *now*, Eric reflected—finding somebody who wanted a rock. Well, he might be able to. You never knew. "What kind?" he asked Mr. Evans in a businesslike manner.

"C'mon in. Ahshow ya."

Eric went in. Mr. Evans lived alone, so there was nobody to make him dust anything, or keep his rock collection from overflowing the windowsill, where it had apparently started, and creeping around the edges of the floor. He knew where everything was, though. After a considering glance around, he shuffled over to the corner behind his shabby easy chair, bent slowly, slowly, with one big knobby hand reaching out ever farther, and finally grasped something in the shadow. Then he reversed the process and eventually shuffled back to Eric, holding a rock the size and nearly the shape of a hockey puck in his palm. It was grayish, veined here and there with a vague pattern of paler lines. It seemed to have little to recommend it.

"Petoshkey shtone. Nah polished," said Mr. Evans with a shrug of his massive, rounded shoulders. "Buh kind unushal. Y'know? Goddin Mishgan."

"Uh—what?" The translation was getting a bit beyond Eric.

Mr. Evans fumbled in his shirt pocket and clapped his hand to his mouth. Then he repeated clearly, "It's a Petoskey stone. I got a couple of 'em in Michigan, two-three years ago when I went back to see my brother. 'At's where they come from, Michigan. Here. I'll show you somethin'." Beckoning with a sausagelike finger, he lumbered over to the window and dipped the finger into a lidless teapot standing on the sill beside a rather straggly geranium. Bringing it up wet, he wiped it gently across the surface of the stone, then displayed the result with a small, triumphant smile.

"Hey, neat!" exclaimed Eric. Where the water had touched it, the stone had darkened to a rich brown-gray, against which the paler lines now showed up dramatically as an over-all network pattern, exactly as though the stone was encased in a little mesh bag. It really *was* unusual.

"You spray 'em with hair spray, they'll stay like that," said Mr. Evans. " 'Swat my brother says. I never tried it myself. Or a-course you can polish 'em if you want. They're a gem rock. Usta make buttons out of 'em."

"It's a good swap!" Eric assured him earnestly. "I've got to go to school now, but I'll—I'll let you know."

"Okay. You know where to find me." Mr. Evans gave a nod and an amiable wave. When Eric glanced back from the outside door, he was putting his teeth back in his shirt pocket.

Next on the agenda—Angel. Provided she wasn't taking off right after school with one of her yakking-partners. Eric worked his way impatiently through the day, left promptly at 3:32, then dawdled. Shortly afterwards Angel emerged from the school building and started down Rivershore as usual. He let her catch up with him at the Lake Street light and, before she had a chance to start talking, asked her if she'd ever seen a Petoskey stone.

"A what?"

"A Petoskey stone. It's a real interesting kind of rock with—"

"No. Listen, guess what? Debbie Clark's cat has got four of the *cutest* little kittens you ever saw! One's white, and one's stripey, and one's calico, and one's gray with white feet and a little white bib, but she's got to give them away because her mother says one cat is more than enough, and I was going to take the little gray one, but *my* mother says—"

It was just no use. Nobody but one of Angel's chosen best friends was up to her weight when it came to a talking match. It had been a slim chance anyway— Angel really didn't seem the type to need a Petoskey stone. Reverting to his usual role of one-ear listener, Eric began to wonder who *would*. A Petoskey stone had a good deal to offer, it seemed to him. It was interesting, and pretty, and not just your ordinary sort of rock at all. You could show it to people. You could use it to start conversations—or weight things down—or crack nuts—or—

"So what d'you think—should I go ahead or not?" Angel demanded, and waited anxiously for his reply.

"Well, uh—" said Eric, but he'd completely lost the thread. That was always the moment she asked her questions; her timing was infallible. "You mean—about the kitten, or—"

"*Kitten?*"

"Well, I was thinking about something else," Eric told her crossly. He had a notion he'd just passed a pretty good idea, an instant before she'd interrupted him. Now he couldn't remember what it was. "What did you ask me?" he said with a sigh.

"If I should go ahead and order the big-sized picture. For my mother's birthday." Angel gave a short, dissatisfied sigh. "I mean she probably knows already that's what I'm doing. I give her the same thing practically every year. I wish it could be a *surprise*."

For once the answer seemed quite simple. Eric said, "Why don't you give her something else, then?"

"Yes, but what?"

Eric gave the problem his attention. "A nice Petoskey stone?" he suggested.

"Oh, *honestly*!" Angel's scorn wiped that off the map.

"Well, how do I know what she wants? Couldn't you sort of—find out?"

"I *did*. I *asked* her. She says she wants a picture of me."

So much for creative answers. "Well, then, order the big-sized picture," Eric said doggedly. He felt like something ejecting replies from a slot, like movie tickets, whenever its button was pushed. Worse, they were right back where they'd started, as Angel proved at once by wailing, "But that's my *problem*!"

Fortunately they had reached Rose Lane. Angel stopped, hugging her books and scowling at him. "Tell you what," Eric said. "I'll think about it. And if I get any good ideas, I'll let you know."

"I bet you won't, though," Angel muttered as she turned away.

Exasperated, Eric walked on, thinking: And even if I did get any, you wouldn't like them, because they were *my* ideas. It seemed to him Angel never really liked anything—except cocktail picks—that wasn't hers already. Unless it was something she couldn't have.

She'd probably trade that cigar box in a minute for something you wanted to keep yourself, but offer her a nice, interesting Petoskey stone and she—

Eric halted in his mental tracks. He should have showed that stone to Angel, and then *pretended she couldn't have it.*

Now he thought of it. At least it was something to remember for next time.

He stopped by the apartment only long enough to dump his books and slather a slice of bread with peanut butter. Eating it as he went, he set off once more, this time toward the Hobbyhorse Shop, in Long Alley behind City Hall.

He remembered the little building as soon as he saw it, though he'd paid it scant attention since the T-shirt graphics shop had moved out two years ago, and had supposed it was still vacant. It was anything but. He stood a moment finishing the last bite of his peanut-butter bread and gazing in some awe at the variety of objects crammed into one small display window. It was impossible to take them in, much less classify them—except as used. Some were lots more used than others, and those, he supposed, were antiques. There seemed to be one of everything in that window, from pincushions to rusty hinges to fancy dresses trimmed with feathers—and the latter looked very used indeed. He'd forgotten what Cholly said the owner's name was, but it was written on the glass of the door, right below the dangling cardboard sign that said "OPEN." Maggie Teggly. He went in. As he did so, a little bell tinkled.

"HI! COME ON IN AND BROWSE, DON'T MIND THE MESS, I'M REPAINTING!" cried a female voice from somewhere in the back of the shop. It was a powerful voice, maybe even powerful enough, Eric speculated, to carry to the back rows of Iron Mountain Elementary Auditorium without the P.A. system, though when that went out assemblies usually turned into pantomine because of the lousy acoustics.

The acoustics were fine in this shop, which was long and high and narrow, plunging back from the alley through several rooms almost as full of things as Mrs. Panek's, though better organized—at least in the two front rooms. The third did seem disheveled, with a stepladder in the doorway and a drifting smell of paint, but Eric didn't venture into it. He browsed as instructed, easily spotting everything Cholly had mentioned, including the photos of naked babies lying on their stomachs. There were several such photographs— brownish, dim, and gloomy—oppressively framed and dominating the wall to his left. There was the old wall telephone, too, set in a ponderous oak box. And the old pop bottles and old tools—besides some wobbly chairs and a display case full of small boxes and toys and oddments. Here and there were several things Eric found already familiar, from Mrs. Panek's. In addition there were things he couldn't identify until he read their tags—a 1922 butterchurn, a hair-receiver (which looked like a small china Frisbie with a hole in the top), a boot-scraper, a match-safe and a fid.

A *fid?* Eric was still staring at this mysterious object —a large, tapering pin as long as his forearm, made of some dark wood—when Maggie Teggly appeared from somewhere in the rear and strode genially toward him, wiping her hands on a rag and spreading a powerful aroma of paint thinner.

"Ah-ha! You're wondering what that is, I'll bet." Her voice effortlessly filled the spaces of the shop, floor to ten-foot ceilings. "Well, so did I, and I'm not sure *yet*, except it has something to do with sailors and rope. Always fooling with rope, those fellas. Tying knots in it and splicing it and coiling it. I think that thing's for raveling it, though I wouldn't like to be quoted. What can I do for you? I'll bet a month's profit you don't want a fid."

"No," admitted Eric, looking up at her and grinning slowly. You couldn't help it—she was just somebody you liked right away, before you even got acquainted. She had bright blue eyes and a bright red face and hair combed any old way and clothes that looked as though she might have grabbed them out of drawers and closets as she hurried past. But her smile was dazzling, exhibiting two rows of white and perfect teeth.

She finished wiping her hands, which were still streaked with apple-green and red, and tossed the rag behind the counter. "Fact is, you don't even look like an antique-hunter to me. They don't usually come so young."

"No, I'm just a friend of Cholly Mutton's," Eric told her. "He and I were sort of talking yesterday, and he said I should come up here and look around."

"Cholly Mutton," she repeated thoughtfully. "That would be that dear man Charlie Merton, who keeps nails and kerosene in treasures I would give my eyeteeth for. He hasn't decided to sell me that tool-carrier has he? Or the Clayton's ginger beer?"

"No—that is, not the tool-carrier. I don't know about the—"

"*Lovely* Old English Stone Ginger Beer bottle—

crown cap, mid-brown, white base. You just don't see that color, not very often. Says 'Clayton's' on the front of it. Charlie's kept his kerosene in it for forty years— he *told* me so. I could get thirty dollars for it in this shop. But try and get it away from him!"

"*Thirty dollars?*" Eric gasped.

"Well, twenty-five. Give or take a buck or so." Maggie Teggly waggled a careless, paint-streaked hand. "That color's offbeat. I don't think my Mrs. What's-Her-Name has one anything like it, either. At least, not any that she bought from me."

Eric swallowed. No harm in asking, he told himself. "Well—uh—what if *I* could get it away from him? Would you give *me* thirty dollars?"

He found himself the recipient of an attentive, bright blue stare. "Nope. I've got to make a living. I might give you fifteen. *If* I made sure my Mrs. What's-Her-Name'd buy it. And *if* you could really get it. Are you figuring Charlie'd give it to you?"

"Oh, no!" Eric felt himself go hot as he realized what she was thinking. "I wouldn't just—come out and *ask* him for something worth all that money! And then sell it for myself!" Indignantly he stared back at Maggie, wondering if he liked her quite as well as he'd thought at first.

After a moment Maggie smiled and perched on the edge of the nearest wobbly chair, which had a cord tied from arm to arm to keep anybody from really sitting down. "Sorry. I misjudged you, O Touchy Friend of Charlie Merton. What's your name, anyway?"

"Eric Greene," Eric told her, still mistrustful.

"What *was* your plan about that bottle?"

"I thought I could swap him something for it.

Something he really, honestly needed. I—I don't know exactly what, yet."

"But you do know you need thirty dollars."

"No, eighteen." Eric suddenly remembered bus fare, to the shoe store and back when he went to buy the boots. "Well, nineteen would be better." As Maggie waited expectantly, he added, "It's for a—special purpose." Then he closed his lips and turned away in what he hoped was a careless, subject-changing manner, to peer idly into the showcase.

"Okay, don't tell me," Maggie said. She stood up. "Go ahead and *let* me suffer and die of curiosity. I wouldn't dream of begging. But let me tell *you*, when it comes to swaps, you're talking to an expert. See anything around here you think Charlie'd really, honestly need?"

Eric glanced around again, and reluctantly shook his head. "This is just the kind of stuff he already has."

"Oh, don't I know it! Only his is better. Well, then, d'you see anything *you* really, honestly need? How about a nice wind-up, just like your grandpa used to play with?"

Maggie flashed her dazzling smile, opened the back of the display case, and took out a rather battered tin beetle, which she wound briskly, then set to scuttling around on the glass counter. Eric couldn't help laughing—it was such a busy, beetle-y little contraption. But he couldn't pretend he needed any such thing. He shook his head again, then suddenly focused on something inside the case, just below where the beetle had whirred to a halt. Now *there* was something he could use. A campaign button, big as life. It said "I LIKE IKE" in big black letters.

"How much is that?" he asked Maggie in sudden excitement.

"The Ike button? Couple dollars. You like *that* better'n the beetle? Well, no accounting for—"

"No! No! But I know somebody who collects 'em. And if he doesn't have one like it . . ." Eric was suddenly back in business. "What would you swap for it?"

"Anything worth two dollars to somebody else. Whatcha got?"

Instead of answering Eric hurried to the back of the room, where he had earlier spotted a stumpy, heavy thing shaped like an iron without a handle, very like the one weighing the stack of *Wall Street Journals* on Mrs. Panek's counter. He pointed it out to Maggie. "I might be able to get one of those. What is it, anyway?"

"That? A sadiron. Your *great*-grandma might've used that, for ironing clothes. She'd 've had two or three, heating on the woodstove, and one changeable handle—like this—" Maggie picked up a semicircle of rounded wood lying nearby "—so she could switch to a fresh iron when the last one cooled off. They sell for two, two-fifty. Don't ask me why."

"So you'd swap one of those for that campaign button?"

"Sure. It's a deal."

"Wow!" exclaimed Eric. Now all he had to do was find out what Mrs. Panek would swap for . . . At that instant, before he even had time to feel a slight dismay, the idea he'd *nearly* had an hour earlier—then lost when Angel interrupted him—sprang back into his mind and solved his problem. At least, it might. "I have to find something out," he told Maggie rapidly. "How late do you stay open?"

Maggie glanced at her watch and laughed. Her laugh was as big and easy as her speaking voice. "I'm already closed. Just been too busy to turn my sign around. Now, don't let that bother you." She put a friendly hand on Eric's shoulder and piloted him toward the door. "I'm open on Saturdays and Sunday afternoon. I'll save that button till you show up. But listen." She halted, pinning Eric with her bright blue gaze. "Once you've done it, and got your eighteen dollars, *then* will you tell me what it was all about?"

"It's a deal," Eric told her with a grin. He waved as she closed the door behind him and turned the sign to "CLOSED." He'd decided once and for all that he liked Maggie Teggly fine.

5

The Big Swap

"Well! Don't you look all fresh and windblown, though!" exclaimed Jimmy's mother as she let Eric in Saturday morning. "Been out running, have you?"

"Not exactly," Eric panted. "I mean, I just had an errand I had to do, that's all." The fact was, he had run all the way to Mrs. Panek's to ask an important question, then all the way back, highly satisfied with the answer, and he had big doings planned for the afternoon.

"Well, take off your jacket—want me to hold that sack for you? What's *in* it, anyway?" Mrs. Nicholson held the tightly knotted plastic bag nearer to the light and peered at it. "Looks like one of my old dust rags."

Eric hung his jacket on a hook, grinning sheepishly. "It's a smell for Jimmy. Is he still collecting them?"

"Good heavens above, I didn't know he'd started!" Mrs. Nicholson gave her little screech of a laugh and handed back the sack as she reached for her coat. "He must have been pleased last night—I let the peas boil over, and *nothing* smells worse." Raising her voice, she cried, "Bye-bye, honey, I'm on my way!" She grabbed her purse, adding to Eric, "Box of cheese crackers on the counter. Oh, and when Mrs. Abbington comes for her alteration job, there it is, and the bill's pinned to it. So long!"

Then she was gone, and Eric, with a glance at the bright blue dress hanging from a cupboard knob, went on into the living room. The first thing he saw was the cut-out ad for the boots, still fastened to the curtain. The table below was strewn with crayons and paper, and Jimmy's wheelchair was pushed up to it, but he was watching eagerly over his shoulder for Eric.

"Did you say you brought me a smell?" he demanded.

"I brought you five," Eric told him, handing over the plastic bag. "Open that one last, it's the strongest. Here, try these first." From various pockets he produced the trimming of leather from Mr. Lee's shop, the garlic clove his dad had brought home as promised, a piece of orange rind, and a little wad of cotton doused with the witchhazel Dad used as an after-shave lotion.

"Oh, wow!" cried Jimmy with his usual enthusiasm, and began to sniff each one in turn, chattering between sniffs. Eric fetched a paring knife from the kitchen to cut the garlic in two, and twisted the orange peel to intensify its scent. Eventually Mr. Lee's highly aromatic old shoe-polishing rag came out of its sack and into play. Even so, in a few minutes Jimmy was sniffing hard, then harder, then complaining in a puzzled voice that even the garlic had lost its smell. "No, *I* have!" he exclaimed a second later. "I remember—Ms. Morgan said I would if I wasn't careful. Now I have to let my nose rest."

Ms. Morgan was the home teacher, to whom, Jimmy explained, he'd happened to mention the smell-collecting on Thursday morning. Friday, she'd brought a volume of the encyclopedia and read aloud to Jimmy much more than he really wanted to know about perfumes and where they came from and how people made them. "Part of it was interesting, though," he admitted as he and Eric preserved each of his smelly new objects in plastic wrap. "Like about ambergris coming from the innards of sick whales—*y-y-yuck!* And did you know cinnamon is a kind of tree bark? And there's a kind of flower called 'ylang-ylang'! Here, lemme read you that part."

He wrestled the encyclopedia from the table onto his thin little lap and began to instruct Eric on the subject of perfumes, while Eric completed the plastic-wrapping and wondered how he was going to measure Jimmy's foot without arousing Jimmy's overactive curiosity. He had waked up this morning realizing that if he actually did find enough money for those boots, he wouldn't know what size to buy.

He was feeling daring but hopeful about his swap campaign. Last night on the way home from the Hobby-horse Shop he had stopped by to see Cholly, ostensibly to report that he had met Maggie Teggly, but really to steal another look at Cholly's kerosene container—the familiar grubby ginger beer bottle he had completely failed to appreciate before—and to study Cholly's shoes. He was pleased to note that the latter were in an advanced stage of dilapidation, and certainly needed re-heeling. But when he had somehow managed to bring this up without sounding too tactless, Cholly only laughed and shook his head.

"Them! They need a good bit more than reheeling, son. They need a new pair!" He stuck a short, stubby foot out and turned it this way and that, examining it critically. "Or mebbe half-soling, and that costs nigh as much! Seventeen-fifty they want for it now! And that's this man-made stuff. Why, I usta get a pair of leather half-soles done for three-and-a-half, includin' shine! But I was workin' for peanuts meself, back in those days. It's all relative. That's what it is, son, relative."

Eric had agreed, and shortly afterwards went on homeward through the gathering dusk, thinking hard. Scratch the reheeling job as a possible swap for that ginger beer bottle. He simply had no swap for it yet— he'd have to trade up to it. So much was certain. What was harder to figure was just how far along he'd be once he traded all the things he did have swaps for. Every time he tried to work it out, he got lost in a maze of possibilities. It was like trying to see around corners. There was only one way to find out where he'd wind up, and that was to start swapping.

By the time he went to bed last night he'd made up his mind to begin—today, as soon as his Jimmy-morning was finished. Everybody was likely to be available on a Saturday afternoon.

Meanwhile, here was Jimmy slamming the encyclo- pedia shut and changing the subject in his usual quick- silver way—back to the drawings he'd been working on when Eric arrived.

"Mom said she maybe could get me some thicker paper, and a box of watercolors if I'd be careful with the water. They'd work a lot better, don't you think so? Crayons are kind of clumsy. Look there—I couldn't do the designs right at all. You can hardly tell what they are." He was spreading his efforts out on the table for Eric to see—half a dozen drawings, large and small.

"I can tell what they are," Eric assured him. They were all pictures of the boots. The most ambitious showed a boy-figure wearing them, though the boy was so sketchy and the boots so lovingly detailed that it was obvious which Jimmy thought more important. "They're pretty good, too. Want to draw some more?"

"No, I'm tired of drawing. Let's play Boggle."

So they played a noisy and hotly contested hour of Boggle, with Jimmy winning three games out of four as he always did. Then they had some milk and cheese crackers, then Mrs. Abbington came for the dress Jimmy's mother had altered, then Jimmy's nose was rested enough to smell his collection again, and the time was going and *still* Eric hadn't figured out how to measure Jimmy's foot. At last he remembered something, and it all became simple.

"Did you know your foot's as long as your fist is big around?" he asked Jimmy idly as he headed for the kitchen with the milk glasses.

"No. Who says?" Jimmy was already making a fist and looking at it calculatingly.

"My dad. If I had a tape measure I could show you."

"Mom's got one! In her sewing basket, right over there!"

So Eric picked up the tape on his way back into the room, and two minutes later the thing was done. It was a big relief, and he enjoyed the rest of his morning. Mrs. Nicholson came back at half-past twelve and invited him to lunch, as she always did, then it was time for Jimmy's rest and Eric's departure. He bounded upstairs to 309, went directly to the little Chinesey box and got out the triangle stamp, and after a last fond study of it, took a deep breath and dialed Willy's number. After that he phoned Steve. Shortly after that he trotted downstairs again and left the building.

His next couple of hours were busy ones. He went first to Willy's and surrendered the stamp. Willy was gloatingly glad to get his hands on it at last and insisted on mounting it in his album immediately, while Eric waited. He would have had to wait some more, long enough to be shown the rest of the stamp collection in slow detail, if he had not convinced Willy that they'd have much more time on Sunday.

"Okay," Willy said at last. "Then come back tomorrow, soon as you can after lunch. And hey—we could do that Language Arts stuff together, you want to?" Willy was weak in Language Arts.

"If you want to do the math together too," Eric said firmly.

"You drive a hard bargain," Willy complained with a grin, but he agreed, and—after being reminded—fetched the Corgi Jaguar and handed it over.

Eric departed, casting a carefully unenvious glance at Willy's bright red Schwinn—only two years old—lying on the grass beside the front walk. He could not see why Willy kept talking about a twelve-speed, when he already had this. Maybe for the same reason he'd switched to stamps from Corgis. He just got bored fast. Anyway, it was lucky for Steve Morris.

Steve lived six long blocks from Willy, around the near end of the lake and halfway up the hill, where the streets had names like Appleblossom Court Way and people's houses had a View. But it was worth the hike. Steve received the Jaguar with a rapture worthy of greater things, went immediately to fetch the thunder-egg and would have thrown in the broken-bladed Swiss Army knife if required to. Eric was satisfied to take the thunderegg and start for home. He was a little anxious about the next swap. *He* considered the thunderegg a beauty—it was as big as his fist, and the cut and pol-ished face showed lovely striations of brown and azure. He could only hope that a rock expert like Mr. Evans would not dismiss it as ordinary.

He need not have worried. After keeping him in anxious suspense for a full two minutes of scrutinizing the offering, then slowly lumbering to the window to study it more closely still, Mr. Evans gave a solemn nod and transferred his gaze to Eric's face. "Nipe 'pecimen," he said earnestly. "Bery nipe color! Glad to hab it."

"Oh, good,!" gasped Eric on a rush of pent-up breath.

"Now you'll want tat Petoshkey tone," Mr. Evans went on benevolently, shuffling across to the corner behind his chair and eventually producing the stone. "Here y'are, then. I'm satispy ip you are."

"Oh, sure, I am! Thanks ever so much, Mr. Evans. I'll—I've got to go now. See you! Thanks again!"

Leaping and bounding with excitement—every-thing was going so well—Eric headed toward Mrs. Panek's shop for the second time that day. From the way she'd answered his question this morning, he was hoping the next swap would go without a hitch.

She had a customer when he reached the shop. Be-fore she finished with that one, another came—some kid Eric didn't know, who took forever deciding between a Mars bar and a Hershey. Finally the coast was clear, and Eric, who had been lurking just outside the doorway, went inside.

Mrs. Panek was still looking gloomily after the candy-purchaser. "That boy's gonna grow up broad as he is tall, and teeth rotted to the roots before he's thirty!" she told Eric. "Don't you ever squander *your* money on candy, candy, candy! You get you an apple or ornj, something that's good for you!"

Since he never had money to squander on anything, Eric felt safe in making this promise, and quickly steered the conversation into more interesting channels. "Mrs. Panek—remember you said this morning you'd swap that iron there if you had something just as heavy to weight your *Wall Street Journals*?"

"Sure, honey, I remember. 'Course, I always kind of liked that old thing—folks ask about it, you know. Half of 'em don't know what it is! Why? You got some idee about it?"

"I've got something I'd like to swap," Eric told her boldly. He produced the Petoskey stone.

"You mean that rock?" she said without enthusiasm.

"Folks'll ask about this, too! I'll show you—if I just had a little water—or some hair spray if you've got any . . ."

He was not surprised to discover that hair spray played no role in Mrs. Panek's life, but water was easy, and she was gratifyingly impressed by what it did to the Petoskey stone. "My *land!* Why, it gets real pretty, doesn't it? And hair spray makes it stay that way? Now, isn't that something!"

"So would you like to swap?" said Eric eagerly.

"Well—I dunno." Her gaze moved doubtfully to the sadiron, and lingered. "That belonged to my own gramma—I've watched her use it, many's the time! And what would *you* do with it, Eric honey?"

"Oh, I wouldn't keep it. But I—I've got a friend who likes them."

"Likes *sadirons?*" Mrs. Panek uttered a laugh as sharp as it was unexpected. "My land, what next! Well, go ahead and take it, I likely won't know the difference by this time next week. Here y'are. Now you come back and see us."

Eric set off in a hurry for the Hobbyhorse Shop, realizing instantly—and rather guiltily—that while the Petoskey stone would no doubt do its job of holding down newspapers, it was nowhere near as heavy as the prize he was lugging now.

Maggie accepted the sadiron without hesitation, handed over the I LIKE IKE button in exchange, and threw in two Indian Head pennies as a bonus when Eric mentioned his friend who collected them.

Eric ran all the way to Mulvaney's, walked briskly through the store with only a passing wave at his dad, who was restocking the deli case, and slid through the employees' door into the backstage regions of the meat department.

"Is Mr. Forrester here?" he asked the new girl at the wrapping machine.

"In the cold room," she told him.

Eric pondered this. He had never before ventured into the cold room, having never had reason to, and he was not quite certain of his welcome. On the other hand, people could stay busy in there for half an hour or even longer. He considered Mr. Forrester's normal manner—brusque but not unfriendly—and decided to take the chance. He eased through the door of the cold room and started along the narrow, shelf-lined aisle toward the hanging carcasses in the rear, zipping up his jacket as the chill of the place struck through it. He found Mr. Forrester checking over a delivery of pork quarters in the second aisle over—an imposing, banker-like figure in an incongruous long white apron and a ravelly cardigan, his rimless glasses on the end of his formidable nose and his breath in a cloud before him. Eric's breath was plainly visible too, and his jeans beginning to feel remarkably thin. Moreover he was suddenly certain he should have waited outside. But before he could retreat, Mr. Forrester turned to peer at him.

"Um?" he grunted. "Yeah? Somebody want me out yonder?"

"No, Mr. Forrester, I—I wanted to ask you something, is all. I thought you wouldn't mind if I . . ."

"Mitch Greene's boy, isn't it? Yeah. Sure. I remember you. Whatcha want, kid?"

"Well, I—Marvin, in the produce, you know—he told me you collect old campaign buttons."

" 'S right." Mr. Forrester rearranged some frozen pork roasts on the shelf with a sound like boards clattering together.

"Well—I've got one for sale in case you're interested." Eric fumbled with stiffening fingers in his pocket and produced the I LIKE IKE button.

Mr. Forrester took it in a large, shapely hand, smiled, and glanced at Eric over his glasses. "Haven't got one of these. So I'm interested. Whatcha want for it?"

Eric swallowed and said firmly, "Two dollars."

"Fair enough." Mr. Forrester jabbed the pin of the button into his cardigan and heaved up the apron to extract his wallet. He selected two one-dollar bills and handed them to Eric. "You come across any other buttons, you bring 'em around. Better get outa here now, it's cold."

He turned back to his work and Eric said, "Thanks! So long! I will!" and hurried back to the semitropics beyond the cold room door.

That was it, then. Mission accomplished. Available swaps all swapped.

He had walked the length of the store and out onto the street before he understood why he wasn't feeling more triumphant—why there was, in fact, a sort of sinking in the pit of his stomach. Leaning against the glass wall of the bus stop on Mulvaney's corner, he stared at the two crumpled bills in his hand.

So. He'd finally let go his triangle stamp to find out where he'd stand when all those swaps were swapped, and he'd found out. Half a dozen swaps = two dollars. That was the end result.

And now he was out of swaps.

After a long, long time—maybe five minutes—he became aware of what he was leaning against, took a thoughtful look at the bus stop sign and another at the big clock on the corner outside the bank. Twenty-seven after four. Slowly he straightened up, folded the two dollars and put them carefully in his pocket, then explored his other pockets to see what was there. He found a dollar and a half—this morning's Jimmy-pay. He watched it dwindle as his mind took little necessary bites out of it: notebook paper, by Tuesday at the

latest. That library fine. The dime he'd owed Willy for a week. It seemed absolutely sinful to spend *ninety cents* of it on bus fare into the city and back. But it was absolutely stupid to go any further with this Great Boots Project—which was going to take longer than he'd thought—without making sure the boots were still there.

There was a pay phone in the shopping mall. That would cost only a quarter. "Hello, this is Eric Greene," he would say to whoever answered at the shoe store. "I want to know if you still have those red-and-black cowboy boots, one hundred percent vinyl, that you advertised in the paper last . . ." "What size?" the salesman would say. And he'd have to say, "Well, I don't know, but his feet are six and three-quarters inches long—better make it seven . . ." "What width?" "Well, I don't know, just sort of normal, I guess—or maybe thinner . . ." "And did you want the scalloped top or the plain? . . . And did you want us to put those back for you . . . And do you have a charge account? . . ."

A Number 37 bus hove into sight around the corner of Evergreen Drive and rattled down Lake Street toward him, looming larger by the second—the last bus that would get him to town before the stores closed. Eric took a deep breath, exhaled explosively, and walked to the curb to get on.

An hour and a quarter later and ninety cents poorer—and, he thought bitterly, not a scrap better off—he was back at the same bus stop, wearily climbing off. It hadn't taken long at the shoe store, once he located it. And the conversation had been almost identical to the one he'd imagined having over the phone. Only there hadn't been a salesman, there'd been a tall young black woman, intimidatingly handsome, like somebody on TV, with big dangly earrings and *seven* bracelets on one arm. Eric had found it almost impossible to talk to her, especially as she kept looking toward the door instead of at him. He had to force himself not to keep looking there too, to find out who she was expecting. At last he had managed to get her attention long enough to point out the boots—they were displayed in a case against one wall along with several other styles. They looked pretty good for $17.99, which was quite a relief, and the young woman, with a parting glance at the door, consented to go back into the stockroom with a ruler and find Jimmy's size.

But she would not save them for him—not even when he offered to put his two dollars down.

"A third down for layaway," she told him, replacing the lid on the box and letting her gaze stray to the door. "Six dollars. Store policy, babe. You got four more dollars?"

"No," Eric told her miserably. "How long will the sale last?"

"Probably 'nother week. You come back Monday, Tuesday. They might still be here."

She turned away, glancing over her shoulder toward the door as she bore the precious box back to the stockroom.

Eric left. Come back Monday, Tuesday—spending another ninety cents to do it—bringing another four dollars he didn't yet have! And they *might* still be there.

Okay, that's *it*, he told himself angrily as he tramped home from the bus stop. It was a dumb, impossible idea in the first place. So forget it. Jimmy'll never even know there was a chance. There *wasn't* a chance.

It was one of those evenings when he was glad Dad wasn't a talker. He veered restlessly between his library book and his weekend homework, finally watched a dumb movie on TV and went to bed. He couldn't decide whether he felt more like bawling or more like hitting somebody. Or maybe it was more like somebody had lied to him—or somebody had died. Whatever it was, it was entirely different—and worse—than just the usual things like not having a color TV or never getting a bike. For some reason he could not fathom there just seemed a lot more *to* it.

6

Gloomy Sunday

Sunday was a bad day for Eric. He woke up an hour earlier than he had the least need to, which would have started any day wrong, and instead of waking rested and hopeful, with a fresh outlook on everything, he felt exactly the same as when he went to bed.

He climbed into jeans and a T-shirt and padded barefoot into the kitchen to pour some orange juice, careful not to disturb his dad, who was still snoring gently behind his closed door. The fat Sunday paper Dad always brought home on Saturday evening lay untouched on the kitchen table like a package under the Christmas tree, awaiting its proper moment, which was when Dad sat down with his coffee. Eric eased the comics out of it and carried them into the living room with his juice, but somehow he couldn't settle down to them, or else they weren't comic this morning, just pointless and dumb.

He finally threw them aside and tried to think— which was pointless and dumb too, because he'd already made up his mind about the boots. Forget them! Nothing else to do. There were times when you just had to admit you were licked. Lots of times. You might not like it but you made your peace with it. No use smashing yourself to bits trying to break through a stone wall. No use trying to climb Mount Everest when you didn't have the equipment. Dad had told him so over and over. Eric had acknowledged it over and over.

Not that he hadn't often argued—silently—with Dad's opinions and advice. Not that he hadn't thought, *Oh, what does he know!* But that was only when he was cross and rebellious, and didn't want to face facts. The facts were that Dad knew a lot more than he did, and usually he was ready to admit that. On the whole he considered he'd jogged along pretty well, making his peace with the way things were, understanding that Dad wasn't well off, couldn't buy things like bikes and there was no use whining about it.

So why couldn't he make his peace with this? He got up angrily from his chair and started shuffling together the scattered comics. Why did he keep feeling so disappointed, just about a dumb little pair of cheap boots?

It finally dawned on him, just as he bent to scoop up an armful of paper. He wasn't disappointed about the *boots*. At least—he was, but that wasn't the problem. He was disappointed in himself—because he couldn't get them.

Well—not exactly because he couldn't *get* them. He mooned over this for a minute, trying to pin it down. Because he'd decided to give up trying?

But that's what you did, when a thing was hopeless. That was the only smart thing to do. Not try to smash stone walls or climb Mount Everest—all that. Dad said . . .

Dad said.

The closed bedroom door opened, and Mr. Greene emerged, tousle-haired, struggling into his old maroon robe. He peered at Eric, up and dressed, raised his eyebrows at this unprecedented sight, and vanished into the bathroom. Eric finished gathering up the comics and took them to the kitchen trash basket, plugged in the coffee, and sat down at the table to waylay his father before the Sunday paper claimed him. Maybe this time what "Dad said" would be something different.

A few minutes later Mr. Greene poured coffee into his favorite blue mug and sat down opposite—then, after a closer look at Eric, turned his chair kitty-cornered, crossed his legs, and propped one elbow on the newspaper instead of reading it. He always knew when Eric needed to talk. What Eric didn't know was how to begin. After a moment, to his own surprise, he bore in from an angle.

"Dad," he said, "you know that time the man from Safeway phoned—'way last year or sometime?" He waited for his dad's puzzled nod, and forged on, not quite sure himself what he was getting at. "Well— wasn't that a kind of good job he was offering you?"

"Dairy foods manager." Mr. Greene shrugged. "A little more money. Lot more hassle."

Hassle. That was a familiar word, too. "I was thinking it was quite a lot more money," Eric said casually.

After a moment his dad uncrossed his knees and turned square to the table, folding both arms on the paper. "I started at Mulvaney's as a box boy my first year in high school. Old Mr. Mulvaney always treated me right. Why should I go work at Safeway?"

Eric could see that. He didn't know why he was asking these questions when they weren't really the ones he wanted answers to, but now he couldn't seem to stop. "I bet you could've been dairy foods manager at *Mulvaney's*. After Mr. Johnson died. Or produce manager! Instead of Marvin."

His father smiled, mostly with his eyes, which dwelt warmly on Eric for a moment, and he seemed about to say something, but instead settled back in his chair and drank some coffee. Eric had hardly expected a reply. His dad knew his feelings on these subjects and had tried patiently to explain before, mentioning hassle, mentioning finding your niche and making your peace, saying he'd had enough ups and downs and backs and forths in his life and preferred it uneventful. Obviously he'd decided not to repeat himself.

Still wandering mentally among a scatter of facts that seemed to have no connection, Eric said, "But you did quit Mulvaney's once—when you went to work at the library. When you went to the University for library training."

"Not the same thing. That was just moving on. To a lifelong career. Or so I thought."

Eric glanced quickly at his father's expression, wary of the flat note that had come into his voice. Why am I giving him all this flak? he asked himself. I'm kind of nagging.

But now might be the chance to solve a mystery he'd never understood. "Dad?" he said. "How come you never went back? To the library job? I mean—they laid everybody off, but then they got voted more money and people got their jobs again—"

"By that time I was working for Mulvaney," Mr. Greene said quickly. He moved in his chair as if he found it uncomfortable. Even more abruptly, he added, "They didn't lay everybody off." He glanced at his paper, then almost pleadingly at Eric. "It's all over long ago. You got a problem you want to talk about? Or—"

Or do I just want to nag, Eric finished to himself. "Not really," he mumbled. "I just—got to wondering. Sorry." He got up, went to the cupboard and got the cereal box and a bowl.

Obviously, the mystery wasn't going to be solved today, either. Or maybe ever, if it was up to Dad to explain. He didn't want to talk about it. Or just— *couldn't.*

They didn't lay everybody off. Was that an explanation? As he munched his cornflakes, Eric tried to imagine being laid off from—well, from Language Arts class, which was his favorite and the one he was best at. Say they had to change that hour to Independent Study because they couldn't pay the teacher. Only they didn't lay off *everybody.* Angel Anthony got to stay, and Debbie Clark and a couple others who always got A's on every single paper. They got to go to the teacher's house and have Language Arts there. But the rest were out in the cold. Okay. Then say the school got money again and the teacher came back, and the rest of the kids could come back if they wanted to. So—would they? Would *I?* Eric asked himself.. How would I feel by that time?

He found he couldn't answer for himself, because after all, Language Arts class was a lot different from a lifelong career, and anyway, how did he know how he'd feel? But he knew how some people would feel— Melinda Jones, for instance, or Willy. They'd get mad. They'd ask everybody in sight how come Angel Anthony got to stay in that class, and they didn't. And even if they knew—(Willy would; he always got C-minuses)—they'd be too proud to go back, or too sulky.

But, thought Eric, groping, but what if they *didn't* know why they'd been—well, weeded out.

That would be scary. It would hurt. It kind of hurt Eric right now, just thinking about it. What if you'd always thought Language Arts (or library work?) was your very best thing? Then you might never go back, because you couldn't risk being weeded out again when you least expected it. Instead you might stick forever to something you *knew* you could do. Do with both hands tied behind you. You might be bored but you'd be safe. Like Dad.

For just an instant Eric saw that vividly, like a landscape in a flash of lightning. Then it all went murky again and he wondered if he'd seen anything at all. He was tired of thinking about it anyhow. And tired of the cornflakes, which had gone all soggy.

"Guess I'll go out and walk around a little," he told his dad, who studied him questioningly a moment, hesitated, then nodded and folded the paper another way.

Outside, it was more like June than early April. Eric unzipped his jacket and let it flap, wishing he'd left it behind. The firs all had little bright green tips on their branches, and the other trees showed a mist of green caught in their bare black limbs. There were azaleas out—just since yesterday, it seemed like, though yesterday he hadn't really been looking. Too busy running all over the place swapping things and trying to climb Mount Everest without equipment.

What's more, thought Eric, suddenly kicking a fallen fir cone so hard it sailed clear across the street, I wish I was still doing that today! Instead of making my peace with this.

Restlessly he swerved and crossed the street after the fir cone, kicked it again and kept it going in a wrathful zigzag until all its stiff little pointy scales began flying off this way and that and there was nothing much left to kick. So. Now I've planted little fir trees all along the Fifth Street sidewalk, he told himself with a half-grumpy, half-amused glance behind him. Old Johnny Firseed. All I need is a fiddle in a green baize sack and a charcoal stove to mend pots and pans.

Pots and pans. Cholly.

Eric looked up from the sidewalk. Less than a block ahead, the dilapidated old house nestled under its huge maple tree like a frowsy chick under a swan—and Cholly never went anywhere on Sunday mornings. Eric swerved back across the street, trod down the sloping path, and stuck his head inside the basement doorway.

"Thought I knew that footstep," Cholly remarked from the workbench, restoring a handful of nails to a coffee can and reaching for his teakettle. "Ready for your cuppa, are you?"

"Okay—if you're not busy." Eric descended the two crumbling steps, dropped down on the hard old daybed, and almost at once got up again and began wandering around, staring at this thing and that without taking much note of what he was seeing, while Cholly went through his tea-making routine and talked about the price of sugar and the trilliums blooming in the ravine and the raccoon he'd surprised that morning nosing around his garbage can.

"Really? A real raccoon?" said Eric, momentarily diverted.

"A real fat rascal, a-wearing his robber mask. I sent him packing, let me tell you. Else he'd bring all his cousins and his uncles and his old maiden ahn-ties tomorrow. You mean you never spotted any raccoon-robbers down around that flat of yours?"

"No, never," Eric answered. Cholly had more to say about it, but Eric's gaze had fixed on the Old English Stone Ginger Beer bottle and his thoughts moved on. At the next pause he said, "I went to that shop the other day, that Hobbyhorse place you told me about."

"Did you now! And how did you get on with Maggie Teggly?"

"Fine." Eric felt a smile tugging at the corners of his mouth in spite of everything.

"Ah. Thought you might. Which cup you want, son, the plain or the fancy?"

"Fancy." Eric accepted his tea in a cup with a gilded rim but only half a handle, and sipped it gingerly. He didn't really care for tea, but had never found a way to tell Cholly so. "I saw the old telephone, and the naked baby pictures and all. And she showed me an old, old wind-up beetle made all of metal—not a bit of plastic on it. It still worked, too."

Cholly chuckled, set his tea mug on the workbench,

and himself on the old carpet-covered stool in front of it. "I'll have to tell me artist friend, Robert Sparrow. He likes wind-ups."

"He collects them?" demanded Eric, suddenly attentive.

"Well, not to say collects. He likes to draw 'em. Don't ask me why, but he'd ruther make a pitcher of them little gadgets than of a nice buncha flowers or a tree or something. He's a got a shelf full of the things— old 'uns, new 'uns, in-between. He'd show 'em to you, was you to stop in there one day. Nice chap. Bit odd, but you got to make allowances for a artist. Lives in Diamond Street, or back from it, alongside that Garden Shop yard where they keep all them little trees in pots. Sparrow's place used to be somebody's garage—maybe still is. But he lives up above."

"Oh—that place. Is it painted yellow? With a little sign on the side?" said Eric, all the while telling himself to forget it, he wasn't going there anyhow, never mind if Robert Sparrow liked wind-ups, he probably wouldn't have a thing to swap, and besides that was all over.

"That's the place. You stop in. Tell 'im I sent you to see all them little scoot-arounds. Care to have that cup freshed up?"

"No, thank you," Eric said hastily. "Cholly— how'd Maggie Teggly ever get started in a shop like that? It seems such a kind of—kind of funny—"

"Don't it? I know what you're sayin'. A real odd business for a young lady—all them old bits and pieces like I use meself. When here we are in this ee-lectronic age. I don't rightly know how she started. But I'll tell you one thing—that shop's what they call a shoe-string operation. Yep." Cholly wagged his bushy head and took a long, expressive slurp of tea. "Hate to say it, but betwixt you and me, I look to see her go broke one o' these days. She can't hardly help it. Too bad. Nice young lady. But impractical, you know. She just don't face facts."

That had an astonishingly familiar ring. Eric examined Cholly all over again, feeling he couldn't quite have seen him before. But there he sat, looking exactly like himself and as different from Dad as anybody could look—yet saying the very same things. Unless I misunderstood, Eric thought. Cautiously, he asked, "You mean—Maggie's trying to climb Mount Everest without equipment?"

Cholly choked on his tea, splashed the workbench setting the mug down, and groped for the old rag he used to clean his tools, coughing into it while turning an alarming crimson—from choking or laughing Eric couldn't tell. As the color faded back into his normal rosy tan, he mopped tea droplets from his whiskers and the worktable with fine impartiality, shoulders shaking and eyes glistening with amusement. "Oh, me, oh, my! Sorry, son. Just hit me funny bone whilst I was swallerin'. 'Tryin' to climb Mount Everest . . .' Now, that's a good 'un! I couldn'ta said it better meself."

"I didn't make it up," muttered Eric. "My dad says it all the time."

"Does he, now. Well, son, he's got his head screwed on. Yessir. You mind what he says—it'll be worth hearin'. I'll wager he knows a thing or two."

Eric nodded reluctantly. But he didn't like the turn this conversation was taking. Not that he'd come here expecting anything in particular . . . he guessed . . .

but he'd have thought Cholly would have given him exactly the opposite advice.

Because—well, *look* at him, he told himself indignantly. Look at this place he lives—and I bet he lives on nearly nothing—but he *likes* it this way. He likes to be *free*, not—not safe and bored. He likes adventure! When he wants to move on, he just goes! Never mind finding his niche. Never mind making his peace, and having enough of ups and downs and hassle. Never mind . . .

"And I'll tell you another somethin' that's worth hearin'," Cholly went on—solemn now, and tossing the rag back on its shelf with an impressive gesture. "You can say what you like about gettin' up in the world. But what most folks are clawin' each other aside for, why it a'nt worth havin'. Success! Bein' boss of somethin'! Lot of cars and clothes nobody needs! Why, you can spend your life just fightin', and get nothin' but a heart attack! Not for me, nossir. I like my peace and quiet." Cholly pointed a work-grimed finger at Eric. "You take a lot of folks, they'll tell you I'm a loser. Oh, I've heard 'em! I see it in their face. But I'm no loser. I'm a winner! I got it made."

Again, Eric nodded. This time it was because he didn't trust himself to speak. It was a terribly mixed-up morning, because instead of being angry, now he felt like crying. And he didn't exactly know the *why* of either one.

A few minutes later he murmured something about homework, thanked Cholly for the tea, and after more or less promising to call on Robert Sparrow one day soon to see all them scoot-arounds—though he doubted he would ever do so—he trudged up the two steps out of the basement dimness and back to the street. The morning was still bright with spring, the maple tree still glorious with all its coppery little leaves unfurling, daffodils still made patches of sunshine everywhere. But Eric's mood was basement-gloomy—even worse than before, he realized, half-bewildered, half-resentful. He was not accustomed to moods, being mostly an even-keel sort of boy, like a ship with a gyroscope built in, but today seemed full of tossing emotions, with himself pitching helplessly about on them, too disoriented to do much of anything but wish it would stop.

He turned on Governor Street and wandered on toward the center of town, tugged by a need he didn't identify until he found himself standing in Long Alley outside the Hobbyhorse Shop—looking straight at the "Closed" sign hanging crooked inside the glass-paneled door. Of course. Sunday morning. Why couldn't he use his head, he asked himself crossly, with his heart dropping like a stone—like an anchor. He wanted to moor right *here* for a while, Sunday morning or not; his ship didn't want to move on. Against all reason and common sense he peered through the glass panel, hands cupped beside his eyes to cut the reflection. He was rewarded by a glimpse of Maggie Teggly in person, briskly sweeping her way—in a quick, uneven rhythm—across the doorway of the farthest room.

Eric's spirits made an instant recovery, leaping like Superman from despair to hope in a single bound. He knocked on the panel—then, as Maggie reappeared, sweeping in the other direction, her mouth wide open and a dramatic scowl on her face, he realized she was singing. He knocked harder. She halted, eyes toward the door but mouth still open, obviously finishing her note, which must have been a high one because he could hear it, like a siren in the distance, from clear outside. She finished a slow, grand gesture, too, then cut off both together with a regal toss of her head, leaned her broom prosaically against the door jamb and crossed the second room to let him in.

"You came to hear my Carmen, now admit it," she said as she unlocked the door. "What I can't understand is how you knew that was on the program this morning. I didn't know myself until I started sweeping out that place back there. The Habanera is perfect sweeping music—especially for getting in corners. What's on your mind, Cholly's friend and mine?"

Cholly is, Eric wanted to say, but there was lots more on his mind than that—so much and so muddled that it was impossible to tell anybody about it, really, and he wasn't entirely sure he wanted to. So he said, "I was just—passing. I forgot it was Sunday."

"Doesn't quite answer my question, but that's okay. Want to help me sweep? I promise not to sing to you."

Eric was glad to oblige, so Maggie relocked the door behind them, led the way into the back room and handed him the broom. "I'd got to about there," she told him, pointing. "You finish, and I'll arrange the dollbabies. How d'you like this room, now it's all fresh painted? It'll be all dolls and toys."

Eric looked around and nodded approval. The apple-green walls looked fresh and springy; apple-red trimmed the window frame, display case, and one straight chair. All the furniture for sale was child-sized or doll-sized; the dolls themselves, plus a jumble of chipped lead soldiers, cast-iron horses and wagons, monkeys on sticks and threadbare teddy bears, were heaped here and there in boxes waiting for Maggie's magic wand.

She dragged one of the boxes over to the case and got busy arranging them on the shelves, while Eric applied himself to the broom. He was glad he'd come— it made him feel better to *do* something. Noticing that Maggie was absently beginning to hum, he said, "I don't mind if you sing at me. Go right ahead."

"Got your ear plugs? It's loud, close up like this. And probably not your kind of thing," Maggie warned him.

Eric didn't think he actually had a kind of thing, and said so. He was sure Maggie's couldn't be louder than Marvin's rock music turned up full blast. And it did start soft and a little bit plaintive, almost like somebody explaining something—with a few stirring TA-DA, DA, DA's between, when Maggie was being the orchestra— but before long the sound was filling the high ceiling and both the other rooms, and maybe the whole out- doors as well, thought Eric, who by this time was standing as if paralyzed, clutching his broom. You really couldn't do anything but listen. When the last notes echoed themselves away and Maggie tossed aside an empty box and dragged up a full one, he said, "I never heard anybody sing like that."

"Never went to the opera then. Not surprising. They're not very thick on the ground around here. Never watched one on TV either?"

"I don't think so," Eric said cautiously. "I'm not *exactly* certain what one is."

"A mellerdrammer with music," Maggie told him. "They put in the music because you'd go out of your mind trying to figure out the plot, and this way you don't have to try. You just sit and listen, and the music's so good you don't care what the story's all about."

Eric absorbed this doubtfully. He was pretty sure he was a story man, himself. Still, Maggie obviously knew a lot about music, and he did not. "Do you sing in operas?" he asked her.

She laughed, but shook her head. "Only on Sunday mornings, in this shop." Her hands slowed on the teddy bear whose furry legs she was arranging. "Oh, but I wanted to, once upon a time!" she added in a voice quite unlike her usual brisk tones. "Studied five years and sang ten thousand scales and spent all my college money chasing that rainbow. Idiotic. I wasn't half good enough and I knew it, really."

Eric watched her apprehensively, braced for the news that it was no use trying to smash stone walls, or climb Mount Everest without equipment, and thinking that if one more person told him that this morning— or anything like that—he'd just . . . well, he'd just simply . . .

Maggie laughed again, and sat the teddy bear in the case. "But I had a great time trying!" she finished cheerfully.

It was as if six bricks had been lifted abruptly from Eric's head—as if he were bouncing around, weightless, like an astronaut. "Honest? Did you?" he said, feeling his whole face spread in a grin that no doubt made him look idiotic himself. "You—you didn't mind not . . . not . . ."

"Well, of course I minded. But you can't have everything, can you? You always get *something*. Even if it's only a good strong hunch you'd do better at something else."

"So you—wouldn't do that way again?" Eric said, feeling the glow fade a little.

"Oh, in a minute! I *am* doing that way again—if you mean holding my nose and jumping, to see whether I sink or swim. You didn't suppose for a minute I know the first thing about running a shop?"

Eric leaned his broom against the wall and his elbows on the display case. "But you *are* running it," he said earnestly.

"So far I am. Beginner's luck."

"Cholly—Cholly says you'll go broke. He says you're sure to."

"Everybody said that at first. Not so many now."

"But what if you *do?*"

"Then I do, Eric Greene, my friend." Maggie leaned on her elbows too, eye-to-eye with him over the display case, smiling a little. "And after that I pick up the pieces and stick Band-Aids on my sore spots and start thinking up something else to try. I won't fail at *everything*, you know. I'm strong and willing, and at least average-smart. I'll get there—wherever 'there' turns out to be."

There was a silence. For Eric, it was full of a gathering excitement in his middle—and a gathering strength, as if he suddenly had more muscles than he used to. Feeling rather short of breath, he asked her, "Do you think *I'll* get there? Anywhere?"

"You? That's the easiest question I've heard to-day. I am absolutely, positively sure of it," said Maggie.

Eric couldn't say a word. He and Maggie kept on looking at each other for a moment, very satisfyingly indeed, and then he seized the broom and finished his sweeping, and she finished arranging the case. When they spoke again it was about where to store the cartons, and after half an hour or so Eric said good-bye and started home.

He was thinking hard as he crossed the Sunday-morning emptiness of Lake Street and headed up Market toward Fifth. That was quite a question he had asked Maggie. And it was quite an answer she had given him. Question and answer both were a little bit silly, he realized that. But they made him feel like somebody new and different, all the same. And he couldn't help wondering—apologetically, because he knew it wasn't exactly fair—what Dad would have said to that question. He was pretty sure he knew.

For the first time, he asked himself consciously if what Dad said could be wrong. Right for Dad, maybe. But wrong for *him*. *He* thought it was more fun trying for *something*, even something impossible, than just quietly giving up. The very idea made him mad. Yes, and getting mad was a help sometimes. Like for instance the first time he'd ever seen Willy Chung, back in about fifth grade. They'd blacked each other's eyes before deciding to become best friends. And he'd been losing that fight—as he remembered very well—until he suddenly got really mad.

Halfway along a daffodil-studded block he stopped in his tracks. *I'm really mad now,* he announced—in silence—to the world at large. *So just look out. Mount Everest, here I come.*

Briskly he stalked the rest of the way to the apartment and up the stairs two at a time. His dad had finished the paper and was in the living room, watching the *Meet the Author* program he always watched on Sunday mornings.

"Eric?" he called. When Eric paused in the living room doorway he gave him one of his quick, thorough glances, then said casually, "Everything okay?"

"Just *fine*," Eric told him. He went on to his own room, astonished at how full of bounce and strength and confidence he felt, when just a couple of hours ago he'd been dragging his tailfeathers in the dirt. Why hadn't he ever done all this before? he demanded of himself. Made up his own mind, thought it out? Why hadn't he *dared* himself to get A's in math, instead of just limply accepting C's? Why hadn't he made some sort of push to get *himself* a bike some way or other, whether Dad could get him one or not? If he'd done that—if he had a bike now—he could already have been earning lots of money, at better jobs, and there'd be no problem at all about the boots! Well. It wasn't too late! He could *still* get a bike somehow, someday, he'd *find* some way to get one.

But first he was going to get those boots. He had one week. Okay. He was starting now, today. He shoved the books off his ring binder, opened it upside down, and began ransacking his brain for new lists.

7

Tackling Mount Everest

They were pretty good lists, Eric thought when he read them over half an hour later. Better than anything he could have thought up early that morning—lots better than after he'd been to Cholly's—and even a *little* better than when he'd left the Hobbyhorse Shop, probably because he'd then got mad.

New all-purpose rule for solving problems: Get mad, he thought. He'd have to tell Jimmy, just to hear him giggle.

But it was true—getting mad had made him *think* harder than before, remember harder, recollect things he'd seen but never really looked at. Like all those little empty bottles on Mrs. Panek's hall closet shelf. Like the box of old photographs in his own dad's bureau drawer. Like a lot of little items in Maggie's front display case that were now reminding him of things he'd noticed elsewhere. Like the notion that somebody besides Mr. Lee might be willing to swap *work* for *things*—and the idea that people might want things they didn't even know they wanted until he, Eric Greene, supersalesman, told them so.

He glanced through the lists again, with a satisfaction suddenly dimmed by the realization that the older items on it, the ones he'd already swapped yesterday, now had to be crossed off. Reluctantly, he did so, materially shortening the lists. Not counting Steve's broken Swiss Army knife and torn box kite and Mount St. Helen's T-shirt—none of which Eric could believe to be irresistible—it left only one item in the original list of THINGS PEOPLE MIGHT SWAP: Mr. Lee's reheeling job. However, he had now added several new items:

> *little bottles—probably antiques (Mrs. P.)*
> *old photos (Dad—and maybe Mrs. P?)*
> *sewing and alterations (Jimmy's mother)*
> *Angel's Between the Acts cigar box (she's got to!)*
> *old wind-up beetle (Maggie)*

And the list of THINGS PEOPLE WANT, in addition to the old leftover "cocktail picks," "cigar boxes," and "smells?" now included some really creative ideas:

> *clothes alteration or repair (Maggie? Cholly)*
> *little bottles and old photos (Maggie)*
> *better birthday present (Angel, for mother)*
> *wind-ups (Cholly's artist friend Robert Sparrow)*
> *some other box to keep cocktail picks in (Angel)*
> *china dogs (Angel's sister's best friend or whoever*
>   *that was)*
> *perfume bottles (Angel's sister)*
> *something Mrs. P. can use to pull down her window blind instead of that little hook-thing which I think I saw one like this morning in Maggie's case.*

He squinted, trying to visualize that case in the second room of the Hobbyhorse Shop. He had walked right past it at the time, his mind on sweeping and *Carmen*, but he'd got a distinct impression of some of those little hook-things on the glass shelf—maybe five or six of them, in a row. He was almost sure one had a pink handle. He had no idea what they were for. But if he hadn't just made them up out of his head (and he would never have invented a pink handle!) then Maggie might welcome another. Might she swap that beetle for it? Maybe. Provided Mrs. Panek would give up the hook-thing in the first place. And *that* was provided he could find her something to use instead, to pull down the blind. And if all that worked, and Robert Sparrow wanted the wind-up . . . and had something to swap for it . . .

Feeling that he was starting at the wrong end somehow, Eric brooded over his THINGS PEOPLE MIGHT SWAP list, which seemed to get shorter every time he looked at it. Nothing on either list appeared to match anything on the other—except, of course, Angel's Between the Acts cigar box and Mr. Lee's reheeling job, and there seemed no way to get them together. Moreover that great creative idea about Jimmy's mother performing magical improvements on Maggie's and Cholly's clothing seemed, on second thought, a little *too* creative to be polite. Eric spent an uncomfortable moment trying to imagine how he would mention the matter to either party, and hastily closed the ring binder and stood up. Never mind being creative; what he needed was some actual stuff to swap.

That meant phoning Angel.

He sat by the phone a minute, putting it off, trying to convince himself it would be easier if he talked to her tomorrow, in person. He failed. If anything, she was less get-at-able in person than on the phone. He looked up the number and dialed.

Angel herself answered on the second ring. Before she could add anything to "hello," Eric said rapidly, "Angel this is Eric Greene and I'm in a big hurry so don't interrupt me for just a minute because I have to know something about that little cigar box you keep your cocktail picks in—and what I have to know is: What would you take for it? I mean—well—swap."

There was dead silence on the other end of the phone.

After a moment Eric said cautiously, "Angel?"

Angel said, "What."

"You can interrupt me now. I mean answer."

"I never interrupt people," Angel said coldly. "I wait until they are finished."

"Well, I'm—I've finished."

"Then I'll answer the same as I answered all the millions and millions of other times you've asked the same question! I do not want to swap that box, I *need* it. Let your friend get one some other place!"

"Okay, okay, I didn't mean to make you mad," said Eric hurriedly. "I just sort of wondered. I mean . . . just pretend for a minute you *did* want to swap it sometime—*then* what would you take for it?"

"Оннннннннн!" Angel exploded, drawing it out into a noise that sounded like a day-old tiger growling. "Eric Greene, I think you must have lost your mind! All right, I'll tell you what I'd take for it! A thousand dollars! Or a ruby and diamond necklace! Or a—a—beautiful gorgeous jewel case, trimmed with solid gold! NOW will you let me alone about that box?"

"I guess I'll have to." Eric sighed, and replaced the receiver. For a while anyway, he added to himself. Somehow with Angel he couldn't put a foot right, no matter how he went about it, but obviously making her mad was not the way. The trouble was, he never knew what was going to make her mad. Maybe the best thing was to wait till he had some substitute box to offer—something really good. Or some great, marvelous idea for her mother's birthday. Or maybe, after all, Mr. Lee would raise his price.

After gazing thoughtfully at the phone a minute, he looked up Mr. Lee's home number and dialed again, hoping people didn't mind being phoned on Sunday. Mr. Lee didn't mind that at all—"Of course not, pal! Call me any time you like!" But as he explained, he couldn't raise his price; the new heels alone cost him more than a Between the Acts box was worth, and he was already throwing in his labor. "Maybe this little girl-friend of yours would ruther have some fancy shoe-laces?" he suggested. "I got some dandies—white with little flowers on."

"She's already got some," Eric said sadly. "Thanks anyway."

Dead end. Neither of those two would give an inch. He'd just have to get the box some other way. Meanwhile he needed *something* to start things moving.

There was still his mother's thimble.

Eric went into his own room, found the Chinesey box, and opened it, trying not to miss the familiar, sky-blue presence of his triangle stamp. After all, he told himself, he could go over to Willy's and visit that stamp whenever he wanted to. He stuck his thumb into the thimble and lifted it out, in the way he had always done it. And instantly he glimpsed the thin, quick fingers, and heard just an echo of that special, delighted laugh that wasn't like anybody else's. Slowly he put the thimble back in the box, drawing a long, unsteady breath. It always shook him up a little, having that happen. But as long as it did happen—could happen— he wasn't ready to give the thimble up.

He closed the box and started to return it to his drawer, then hesitated, considering it through narrowed eyes. *A beautiful gorgeous jewel case trimmed in solid gold.* If you deglamorized that by about half to allow for Angel's usual exaggeration . . . and maybe tried some soap and water . . .

He dumped the thimble and the tissue-wrapped agate onto the dresser top and took the box to the bathroom, where he washed it carefully with a cloth. That helped. But the outer, Chinese-red lacquer with its circular gold design still didn't shine like the black interior. Reluctantly Eric decided that he couldn't expect it to. People had handled this box—lots of people. It was old.

Old. So what was wrong with old? Everything in Maggie's shop was old. What you did was call it *antique*.

A beautiful antique Chinese lacquer jewel box with a mysterious design in gold.

It sounded good.

He swallowed, thinking of Angel, wondering if it would sound good to her—if anything would. The very idea gave him a sort of stage-fright, made him want to turn around and walk quickly in another direction.

Well, you can't do that, he told himself crossly. You have to find some way to handle her.

That had a familiar ring. Hadn't he already thought of some new way to handle her? Yes, he had—the other day after she'd rudely rejected his Petoskey stone. *Show her something then pretend she can't have it.*

Now I remember it, he reflected disgustedly. And I've already phoned.

The sound of the canned Big Ben chimes that ended the *Meet the Author* program floated in from the living room. It was chopped off in the middle and replaced by his father's voice. "Hey, Eric. Want some lunch?"

"Oh. Lunch?" Could it possibly be noon? Eric's stomach growled in answer. He called, "Yeah, okay, I'll be right there." Swiftly he returned the thimble and the tissue-wrapped agate to the Chinesey box, and the box to the drawer—for now. Until time to show it to Angel and try the new approach.

And if it works, he thought, I'll need a new box myself.

There was a little match box, nearly empty, that had been knocking around the living room ever since Dad had quit smoking three years ago. That would do —at least for the agate. As for the thimble . . . Eric shut the drawer and headed into the kitchen. He'd been getting a sort of notion about that thimble, and it seemed like a better notion than just selling it to somebody who'd sell it again to somebody else. He'd been thinking about giving it to Jimmy's mother—not quite yet but sometime soon. She needed a nice thimble—hers was only plastic. She would really *use* it, in her sewing. And he could go visit it, even stick his thumb in it, whenever he wanted to—same as he could visit his triangle stamp.

Which reminded him he'd promised Willy he'd come over right after lunch, to look at all the stamps and do Language Arts and math besides. Good, thought Eric, getting the mustard out of the refrigerator for the wienies his dad was dropping into a pot of water. Math would at least keep his mind off Angel and the new approach. And after he got through at Willy's there'd still be time to walk down Diamond Street past the Garden Shop, and see if it was Robert Sparrow's sign on that yellow garage.

At four-fifteen he was standing in front of the yellow garage. It was set back from the street at the end of what had once been a driveway, but was now a paved courtyard bounded on one side by the Garden Shop yard, which was bright with blooming plants for sale, and on the other by a pinkish brick wall which looked the same age as the garage. Beyond the brick wall and a row of trees was the vast Safeway parking lot. It was a funny place to live, but Eric liked it.

He liked the sign even better. It was nailed to the siding beside the big overhead door, at the foot of a flight of wooden stairs that climbed the outside of the garage. It was made of one big weathered shingle, sort of frayed artistically at the thin edge. It not only said "Robert Sparrow" in scrawly yellow letters that looked like a signature, but also showed three little painted sparrows peering at the name. Eric just stood there grinning at it, his ring binder sliding off balance under his arm. He managed to catch that before it fell, but couldn't catch several papers that slithered out of it, along with his math book, which slapped down on the cement walkway with a report as loud as a rifle shot in the Sunday afternoon quiet.

Eric gave an embarrassed glance around as he scrabbled for his belongings, but saw nobody except a couple of old ladies browsing in the cyclone-fenced Garden Shop yard. He hadn't thought to look *up*; therefore he jumped when a voice from somewhere above his head said, "Need some help?"

A young man with a toothbrushy blond moustache was peering down at him from a sort of roof-balcony at the top of the stairs. He held a coffee mug in one hand and his elbows rested on the wooden railing between two potted geraniums.

"No. Thanks. Sorry. I've got it all now." Then, because the young man's face looked both friendly and un-busy, Eric added, "Are you Robert Sparrow?"

"That I am."

"I like your sign—with the sparrows on it."

"Do you? Well, I was just lucky to have a name like that—easy to draw pictures about. What's yours?"

Eric told him, feeling it to be terribly ordinary—though not, if you wanted to get literal, entirely colorless.

"You could draw pictures about that, too," Robert Sparrow assured him. "It would make a fine signature for a painter—just a slash of green. Do you like paintings?"

"I don't know anything about them," Eric confessed. "But my friend Cholly Mutton—I mean, Charlie Merton—"

"Ah! You're a friend of Cholly's!"

"Yeah. He told me you're an artist."

Robert Sparrow considered this as he took a sip of coffee. "Well—I draw pictures," he said carefully. "Sometimes it's not the same thing, you know."

"I know," said Eric, who sometimes drew pictures too.

The young man's grin was wide and sudden, and made his eyes narrow into slits. He didn't say what had amused him, but inquired, "Does this vertical conversation strike you as just the teeniest bit inconvenient?"

After an instant's startled pause, Eric rubbed his neck, which he'd been wanting to do for some minutes, and admitted that it was getting a little stiff.

"Then why don't you come up to my level—since I'll bet Cholly sent you to call on me."

"He—he said you might show me those little scoot-arounds. Sometime. If you weren't a bit busy."

"Well, I'm not a bit busy right now, so come right up." Robert Sparrow poured the rest of his coffee into the nearest geranium pot, adding, "They like it, you know. Caffeine addicts, every one of them!" and turned away, out of sight.

Eric got a firm grip on his ring binder and climbed the stairs. Across the balcony, on his right, a door stood open; passing a window on his way to it, he glanced in, then stopped and stared. Hanging in the window was a sort of bulletin board, covered with drawings thumbtacked to the cork. They were portraits of children of all ages—just the heads, in full-face, profile, or three-quarter view—drawn in crisp black pencil with a few strokes here and there of clay-red. In the lower left corner of every one was outlined a tiny sparrow. They were very, very good, it seemed to Eric. A little awed, he walked on, through the open door, across a space holding a closet and the bulletin-board window, to an inner door where Robert Sparrow stood hospitably waiting.

Hesitantly, Eric stepped in. The apartment was all one long, bright, airy room, smelling of paint the way a garden smells of plants and earth. There was almost no furniture, but plenty of space and lots of pictures. Pictures were hung or thumbtacked helter-skelter over every available wall space, propped on easels, taped to a big drawing board in the front of the room. Nearly all were pictures of children—not just heads, but full-length figures running, digging, sleeping, climbing, swinging, squatting to stare eye-to-eye with a dog or bird or squirrel or flower. One little girl was flying— just soaring on her own, arms outstretched, with tree-tops below her. She looked absolutely at her ease. Some of the pictures were colored, some drawn in pencil, some looked unfinished. All the finished ones had the tiny quick-sketched sparrow in the lower left hand corner, which Eric decided was the way Robert Sparrow signed his name.

The front wall of the room, above a big drawing board, was covered with entirely different pictures, which Eric didn't understand at all. He couldn't tell what they were pictures of—certainly not of children. Most of them were divided into a sort of grid of un-equal spaces, with each space filled by an object or gadget or . . . some sort of little . . . well, *that* one looked a bit like the front end of a bus, a sort of fat bus with big headlight eyes. And could that one be a *cow*? Eric stepped closer to peer at it, and out of the corner of his eye saw Robert Sparrow grinning his sudden grin. He also finally noticed that every single object in every

space in every grid showed somewhere a big wind-up key.

"The little scoot-abouts!" he exclaimed. And now, as if some sort of mental gear had shifted, he could identify them easily—a donkey, a tractor, an outsized mouse, a circus wagon, a drummer—all full-faced to the viewer, all either squashed or expanded to fit their squares. Yet when you backed off, the whole picture looked like a complicated quilt or something, just patterns and shapes, with color flickering all over in the most fascinating way. Eric liked these pictures better than the children now—lots, lots better. He turned to Robert Sparrow, wanting to say so, and found he didn't need to. The artist was watching his face, half-smiling, and nodding as if he already understood.

However, all he said was, "You got it. The little scoot-abouts. Want to see the originals?"

"Yeah! You mean the toys? Yes, please."

Robert Sparrow, who had been leaning in the doorway while Eric inspected his room, turned to a built-in cupboard behind him and opened it, releasing more painty smells and revealing shelves filled with bottles and crumpled paint tubes and bouquets of brushes and stacks of paper, and one whole shelf crowded with wind-up toys. Eric saw the cow right away, and the bright red bus, and what looked like a hundred others. Few of them appeared new. "Wow!" he whispered. "I never *saw* so many. Where'd you get 'em all?"

The artist plucked a small, especially worn-looking metal rabbit from the back of the shelf, wound it up and set it on the floor. It hopped sedately in a circle, its mechanism buzzing loudly, then slowed, and toppled over. "This was mine, when I was about half your age," he said. "I still had him when I was twice your age, and one day I drew his picture. I had some others by then—I always did like wind-ups. They make me laugh. I just—went on from there. I guess I'm crazy."

Eric suddenly remembered why he had come. "Do you have any beetles on that shelf?" he asked.

"Beetles?" Robert Sparrow's eyebrows, which were blond and toothbrushy like his moustache, drew together as he looked over his collection. "I don't think so. A cockroach, yes. A butterfly, yes—a couple. Beetles, no. Have you got a beetle you want to get rid of?"

"Not get rid of, exactly." Eric said cautiously. "More like—swap? I mean, I don't exactly *have* it, but I know where I can get it for you. It's a—a sort of antique. And funny. I think you'd like it."

"I'll bet I would. But if it's a sort of antique I doubt if I have anything valuable enough to swap. Do you know I've been offered a hundred dollars for that rabbit?"

Eric's mouth fell open. He had never asked Maggie the beetle's price and now realized he had no idea what sums he might be talking about—if he could ever get the beetle, if any amount of swapping would do the trick. He had a sudden sensation of being in over his head, way over. He also realized it *was* a trick he was pulling on Robert Sparrow, though he hadn't intended that at all.

"Actually the beetle's for sale to anybody," he blurted, feeling confused and dishonest and ashamed and cross, all at the same time. "At the Hobbyhorse Shop. You don't need me to get it. You could just go buy it yourself."

"Well—thanks for showing me the wind-ups—and everything," he said. "I'll find out about the beetle. Could I come by after school—maybe Tuesday—and let you know?"

"Not Tuesday. I teach at the art school in town on Tuesdays and Fridays."

Since Mondays, Wednesdays and Saturday mornings were Jimmy-days, that didn't leave much. Eric said, "I have a sort of job too. But I'll get here sometime."

"Whenever you can." Robert Sparrow gave an enigmatic smile and said surprisingly, "I may have a job for you myself sometime."

"A job?" Eric echoed.

"Well, a sort of job. Just tell Cholly he was right again."

Without adding anything to this mysterious remark he steered Eric to the door and turned away, leaving him to descend the outside stair feeling puzzled but interested, hoping Cholly would tell him what the artist had meant. Meanwhile, he had another item to add to his What People Might Swap list—if he could think of anybody who'd want it—and if he could acquire the beetle to make the swap.

8

Jigsaw Juggling

All day Monday, Eric's two ill-fitting lists zigzagged around his brain like a jigsaw that wouldn't come together. He wondered if anybody had a china dog or a perfume bottle and wanted a Mt. St. Helen's T-shirt instead. He wondered what Maggie might take for the beetle. He wondered if Mrs. Panek's little hook-thing really was the same as those he'd seen in Maggie's shop. He tried to think what people usually used to pull down shades. He eyed Angel warily from a distance, wondering how she'd feel about a beautiful antique Chinese lacquer jewel box with a mysterious design in gold—but he avoided her. After school, as he watched her go off with Debbie Clark, he even wondered if Jimmy might possibly like one of Debbie's free kittens instead of boots—provided the doctor would let him have one.

He dumped his books at home and went slowly downstairs to the Nicholsons' apartment, wishing he'd find Jimmy all fired up about some new project that had made him forget about the boots. But the ad was still pinned to the curtain, there were several new boot drawings around, and the home teacher had

brought a big book about cowboys that Jimmy was avidly reading. It seemed futile to offer him a kitten—especially since he was probably allergic to cat hair, same as he was to dogs.

Anyway—Eric suddenly realized—the boots themselves weren't quite the point any longer. Somehow, over the weekend, things had got beyond that. The point was *getting them*—and staying with it until he had.

He put it out of his mind and told Jimmy all about Robert Sparrow and the child-drawings and the wind-up pictures, and promised to ask for some painty smells next time he went there. They played rummy for most of the afternoon; Jimmy had made up some new rules to make it harder, and it was—though not for him. Out of eight games, Eric lost six.

He was climbing back up the stairs at five-forty before he even thought to wonder if the boots were still available. They might easily have been sold by now. Half-hoping they had been, he hurried up the last of the flight and phoned the shoe store. It had already closed.

Frustrated, he finished his homework, ate his dinner, watched the news and, feeling as if the day had gone on forever, went to bed as soon as he decently could. He was glad to shut the world off and quit trying to make squarish puzzle-pieces fit into roundish holes. He hoped tomorrow would be more like days used to be. He could hardly remember what it was like before he'd started trying to get Jimmy those boots.

Then, just before he slept, his mind turned one piece of the puzzle upside down.

He awoke Tuesday morning with his whole plan

neatly in place. He sat straight up in bed, wide awake and with his heart pounding as if he'd heard a thunderclap. He could hardly believe it—but there it *was*. The whole thing. Beautiful, logical, perfect, in parade-like procession from A to Z.

If he could just get everything to work.

Drawing in a long, steadying breath, he climbed out of bed and into his clothes. It was going to be a busy day.

He started with his father, at breakfast. "Hey, Dad? You know that bunch of pictures in your drawer? The ones with the rubber band around them, that used to be Grandad's?"

His father nodded, eyebrows raised, and waited for clarification.

"Well—do you want 'em? I mean, all of them? Are there any extras, or spares, or some you don't specially care about?"

Mr. Greene looked baffled, but gave the matter his consideration while he chewed. "Might be a few duplicates—Grandad's sister's collection is all there too." After a moment he added, "I don't even know who some of the people are. Don't care about those. You need old photos for something?"

"Maybe," Eric said, hoping his dad wouldn't ask for what. By now he didn't want to tell anybody anything about the swapping project and the boots. They had somehow become personal, private property. His dad, who was studying him curiously, appeared to be reading some of this in his face, for he ended up asking nothing. Emboldened, Eric ventured, "Would you—you wouldn't have time to pick those out, would you? The ones you don't care about?"

"Before work?" His dad glanced at the clock doubtfully, but said, "I'll make time. You fix the kitchen."

So while Eric washed their plates and got their lunch sandwiches out of the refrigerator, Mr. Greene disappeared into his bedroom, emerging a few minutes later with half a dozen brownish, curling studio portraits, plus a couple of smaller pictures surprisingly heavy for their size. One showed—dimly—an indignant-looking bearded man in a military uniform, the other a pale woman with smooth dark hair parted severely in the middle.

"Daguerreotypes," he told Eric. "That's a Civil War uniform. But I don't think those folks were even our kin."

"So I can have some of these? Or all of them?" Eric asked eagerly.

"Help yourself." Mr. Greene gave his slow, warm smile as he shrugged into his jacket. "See you tonight."

Eric stowed the photographs in his own drawer, feeling that the day had made an auspicious start. Then he took out the Chinesey box, emptied its contents into the drawer, and slid the box into his jacket pocket before hurrying off to school.

He tackled Debbie Clark next. Since she was in his first-hour class it wasn't hard to arrange.

"I heard you have some kittens," he said, pausing by her desk on his way to the pencil sharpener.

He had her immediate and eager attention. "You want one? You want *three?* Oh, please want one— they're so cute, but my mom says we have to get rid of them *this week.* Or else," she finished dolefully.

"Well, I might. Could I sort of take a look at them? Like today after school?"

"During lunch hour, if you want!"

"Lunch hour?" Eric needed only an instant to see the time-saving advantages of this offer. "Okay, meet you by the side door right after the bell."

He had to eat his sandwich as they walked to Debbie's house, first down Rivershore in the opposite direction from his usual route, then along Marina Drive, which curved around the narrow end of the lake. All the houses had their backs to you along there. You could only see their garbage cans and three-car garages. He followed Debbie down a narrow cement walk between two of the garages, and into a utility room, which turned out to be on the second floor. Presumably the rest of the house was below, on the lake level; he caught a glimpse of sparkling water and an expanse of deck. But the kittens were up here.

"Look! Aren't they *darling*?" Debbie said emotionally, catching up a little gray-striped character who had been stalking his brother's tail. "This one's Stripey and that one's Snowflake and the one in the basket is Captain Hook—"

"Captain *Hook*?"

"Well, he sort of scratches. I'm sure he'll outgrow it," Debbie added quickly. "And there's a kind of calico one, mostly white—there, behind the dryer. That's Scraps. Here, Scraps, here Scraps, here Scraps, come here, honey-bunny, oh, aren't you the sweetest little darling sugar-pie . . ."

Eric tuned her out. The kittens were as irresistible as kittens always are. He was a pushover for them himself. But he was trying to see them through somebody else's eyes, and judge them with somebody else's

possible prejudices in mind. "Which ones are male and which are female?" he asked Debbie.

"We *think* Captain Hook's a male. And Stripey. We're almost sure."

Eric picked up Snowflake and stared earnestly into his/her wide, opaque-blue eyes, which were just beginning to show a hint of proper catty green. Are you the one? he asked her silently. How do I tell? He noticed the homemade toy she had been playing with— a wooden ring on a string—put her down, and began trailing the toy in front of her. She reacted instantly, dancing along behind it making lightning-fast swipes with first one front paw and then the other, suddenly pouncing and capturing it before Eric could jerk it away. By now he was laughing and saying things almost as silly as Debbie's sweet-talk. He shut up and straightened, letting Snowflake keep the wooden ring.

"I'll take the white one," he said before he could change his mind. A moment later he broke into Debbie's passionate gratitude and congratulations by adding, "Could I take that toy, too?"

"Oh, sure! But she'll play with *anything*. Like feathers. She *adores* feathers. And she's smart! Why, the other day I—"

"You don't need to go on talking me into it," Eric said kindly. "I've decided. Only thing is, I can't take her until Thursday. Is that okay?"

Debbie eyed him. "Well—if you *promise*—"

"I promise. Honest. Hey, we better start back."

"My mom'll bring me. I've got to eat my lunch. You'll *sure* get Snowflake on Thursday?"

"Sure. Positive! Right after school! So long."

Eric bounded up the walk to the street again, and headed back toward Rivershore and school, feeling triumphant and scared in about equal parts, and hoping he had not just become the sole and permanent owner of a white kitten. His dad didn't care for cats.

At 3:40 he let Angel catch up with him as he stood waiting for the Lake Street light. She started talking before she quite got to him.

"Hey, Eric! I hear you took one of Debbie Clark's kittens! I thought you said you couldn't have a cat because your dad . . . How come you chose the white one? I like the stripey one best, I think he has the prettiest eyes. Are you going to call him Snowflake, like Debbie did? That's a kind of dumb name, I think. My sister said she'd name it Minimal if it was her kitten. You get it? Minimal? I didn't at first, but she says her art teacher at Iron Mountain High says there's a whole school of artists who paint pictures that're just all white, or all black or all gray or something, and they're called "Minimalists." I don't know why they do that, it sounds dumb to me. If I was going to paint a picture I'd want it to be *of* something. A tree or something. I—"

It was just as if they'd never had a hostile telephone conversation. One thing you had to say for Angel, she never stayed mad. On the other hand, she'd probably get mad again, just as fast or faster, if he so much as mentioned her little box. Maybe if he so much as mentioned *any* little box, he thought with a sudden clutch of stage-fright, feeling as conscious of the little Chinesey box in his jacket pocket as if it were radioactive and outlined in pink neon.

The moment had almost arrived to bring it out—

to put his whole scheme to the test. He swallowed hard. What if it didn't work?

All at once the thing fell apart on him. His perfect, logical, A-to-Z plan seemed utterly silly, wobbly, ridiculous. Every single bit of it depended on every other bit, and not one of them was certain or even especially likely. He must be going bonkers, as Cholly would say. He was losing his sense of perspective, as Dad would say. He must've already lost his grip on plain common sense to think nothing mattered except those boots. Better quit right now, before he went any further. He could tell Debbie he'd changed his mind about the kitten. He could forget about the box. No use banging his head against . . . But *that* was what Dad would say, too.

In fact, everything he'd been thinking was just what Dad would say—what Dad would be thinking if it were Dad's plan, and Dad's project. I wasn't going to do that, Eric reminded himself, feeling bewildered but draggingly uncertain. Dad knew more about life than he did—he *must*. Maggie would probably say, "Ahh, what've you got to lose?" But Maggie was kind of impractical. Wasn't she?

"—so d'you want to go with us?" Angel finished, and waited. "I have to know pretty soon," she added impatiently. "Because of Daddy making the arrangements and all. He told me to find out today."

"I—I—" I'll just say I don't want to go, Eric thought hurriedly. Wherever she's talking about. No, I'd better say I *will* go, then try to find out . . .

"You haven't even been listening," Angel accused him, stopping in the middle of the sidewalk.

"No." Eric sighed. "I was thinking."

"You mean about the May Day picnic?"

"No. Why would I be thinking about the May Day picnic?"

"Because that's what I've been *explaining* about! My daddy can borrow a big van from where he works, to take a whole bunch of us, and if you want to go—"

"Oh. Yeah! I'd like to. Thanks. Let's see—that's . . . what day is the picnic?"

"*May Day*. The first of May," said Angel, slowly and distinctly, staring Eric in the eye. "Sometimes I wonder about you, Eric Greene."

"Yeah, me too," Eric muttered.

They turned and walked on. Angel said, "What *were* you thinking about, then?"

Eric made no conscious decision, one way or the other. He simply said, "My botanical collection," and stepped over to a little tree they were passing, frowned at it consideringly, and plucked a leaf.

"Botanical collection? I didn't know you had a botanical collection," said Angel. "What are you going to do with it? What kind of stuff are you collecting?"

"Botanical stuff," Eric told her. He came back to the sidewalk, sliding the Chinesey box out of his pocket with a hand he kept somehow steady. Unhurriedly he removed its lid, dropped the leaf into its shiny interior, put the lid back on, and with his heart dropping like a stone, returned the box to his pocket.

"Where'd you get the box?" asked Angel.

Eric's heart climbed back to its usual position. "This?" he said casually. He produced the box again, giving a careful rub to the gold-lacquer design as he held it for Angel's inspection. "Somebody gave it to me a long time ago to keep things in. It's sort of an antique."

Angel's eyes widened. *"Really?"* She looked dubiously at the box. "I thought antiques were like silver teaspoons, and furniture and stuff."

"There's all kinds," Eric told her. He crossed two fingers of the hand clasped around his schoolbooks, because he was about to tell a whopper. "The lady who gave this to me called it a beautiful antique Chinese lacquer jewel box with a mysterious design in gold."

Angel looked from the box to his face then back at the box—still dubious, in fact downright skeptical. "It just looks like a kind of worn-out lacquer box to me."

"It does to most people," Eric said. "Unless they know a lot about antiques."

Angel thought about this, then inspected the box again. "Of course it's awfully *pretty*," she said. "Really *different*. I mean, the more you look at it . . ."

"It's handy to keep things in, too," Eric remarked.

"Yeah. It's just the right size for my cocktail picks." Suddenly Angel's eyes flew open; she fixed Eric with a bright, suspicious glance. "But you needn't think I'll swap my little cigar box for it, because I won't!"

"Oh, I wouldn't swap *this*," said Eric just as quickly. "I meant to tell you—I guess I don't want the cigar box now. My friend who collects them thinks he can get one somewhere else. He says they're pretty common."

"Oh," said Angel.

"Well, here's where I turn off," Eric added briskly, halting at the Third Street corner. "See you tomorrow."

"Where you going?" Angel stopped too.

"Just over to Diamond Street. To see my artist friend. That is, if he's home."

"Your artist friend? A *real* artist?"

"Yeah, sure. Robert Sparrow. He illustrates kids' books and things. I've seen some of 'em—right there in his studio. He's got whole walls full of drawings." Absently, Eric added, "He's going to draw my picture sometime."

"Really?" Angel was impressed. "Hey, can I go with you to see him?"

Eric let his expression cloud over with uncertainty. "Oh—I dunno. He might not exactly . . . I mean—"

"Pooh, he wouldn't mind!" exclaimed Angel, sure as always of her welcome anywhere, by anybody. "I'm coming along."

"But he might not even be there!"

"So? We can find out, can't we? Come on."

She started energetically down Maple Street, her forelock bouncing, leaving Eric to follow, which he did with an artistic air of having been overruled against his better judgment.

"How come he's going to draw your picture?" Angel asked as he caught up with her.

"I dunno, he just offered to. He does lots of portrait drawings of kids. Charges twenty dollars for them usually. I thought I'd give mine to my dad for Christmas or something." He crossed his fingers again.

"Good idea," Angel said vaguely. Other people's plans and parents weren't quite real to her; Eric had often noticed it.

He added, "Instead of a school picture. I didn't bother with those. And since Robert Sparrow wanted to draw me anyway—"

This penetrated. Angel turned to him with an arrested expression. "Heyyyyyy! D'you s'pose my mother might like one for her *birthday*? Wonder if he'd draw *my* picture?"

"I guess so—for twenty dollars."

"Oh." Angel's enthusiasm cooled. "The school ones are only fifteen—and you get all those wallet-sized ones along with the big one."

"That's true. Better stick with those." Eric waited a moment before adding carelessly. "*My* school photos never turn out any good."

Angel didn't reply, but he could see her remembering that her last ones hadn't, either. She had complained bitterly at the time that they made her look like a baby seal. She'd had her hair cut into that forelock shortly afterwards. "Of course, I might not think the drawings were any better," she said rather crossly.

"No," Eric agreed. Then, as they reached the Garden Shop courtyard, "Here's your chance to find out!"

Angel stopped in surprise. "He lives *here*?"

"Up there—above the old garage. Come on."

He led the way up the stairs, whistling, trying to act as if he came here all the time. Since it was Tuesday, one of Robert Sparrow's days to teach in the city, he was not afraid of intruding. As they passed the roof-balcony window he stopped, pointing to the display of portrait drawings inside. "That's the kind he does for twenty dollars. I think they're real good, myself."

"Wowwwww!" Angel breathed. "So do I!" She pressed her nose against the glass. "Hey! There's Martha *Gettner*! The one up there in the top corner! It looks just *like* her!"

"I don't know Martha Gettner," Eric said.

"She's in my dancing class," muttered Angel. She was still scanning the portraits, one by one, but apparently found nobody else she knew. She turned away abruptly. "Let's go in! I like those! I bet my mother'd just love one for her birthday. I wonder if he'd make me one for fifteen dollars instead of twenty? I don't *have* to order the school pictures. Eric, d'you think he'd—what's the matter?"

"I don't think he's home," said Eric, who had already knocked once on the door. He knocked again, louder.

"Oh, *no!*" Angel wailed.

"I told you he might not be." Eric shrugged. "Never mind, I'll ask him about it, next time I see him. Maybe next week." He started back down the stairway.

"Next *week?* Why not tomorrow?" demanded Angel, clumping hurriedly after him.

"I have my job tomorrow. I suppose I could come by Saturday afternoon, if you're in a big hurry or something."

"I am! I want to *know!* Ask him Saturday, then, okay? Promise?"

"I promise to *ask* him. I can't promise what he'll say."

"Okay," Angel agreed reluctantly. "But phone me *right away*, as soon as you find out!"

"I'll try. Well—I've got to go look up stuff in the library. You can come along if you want, but I may be a while."

"Oh. No thanks," said Angel, as he had known she would. With a last frustrated glance up at the artist's balcony, she started toward home, and Eric headed in the other direction, walking buoyantly on the balls of his feet.

That wasn't really a lie, he was assuring himself. He really *might* drop by the library—after a quick visit to the Hobbyhorse Shop to ask Maggie Teggly some questions. A lot depended on the answers, but the past hour had made an optimist of him, and done wonders for his self-confidence. Then, tomorrow morning on his way to school—if Maggie's answers were the right ones—he'd make a three-block detour into Diamond Street and ask Robert Sparrow a question too. And when could he talk to Mr. Lee? Tomorrow afternoon was Jimmy-day. All right—tomorrow at lunch hour he'd go see Mr. Lee. And after that, Angel again, at school. That left only Cholly to call on—to proposition, to convince—before the action started Thursday.

He felt like somebody trying to organize a troup of untrained acrobats into one of those tidy pyramids, with everybody standing on everybody else's shoulders. Untrained? They were blindfolded. He could only hope they'd hold their poses long enough for him to climb on top.

His steps slowed a little as he examined his own thoughts with a touch of uneasiness. He didn't want to *trick* anybody. Not his friends. He reviewed his plan one last time, and the people involved in it: Maggie and Cholly and Mrs. Panek, Mr. Lee and Robert Sparrow— Debbie and Dad. No, he wasn't tricking a single one. And so far everything was going perfectly—going his way, for a change. Angel he had in the palm of his hand.

Am I tricking Angel? He put the question severely to himself.

After a moment he answered it, just as severely: Yes. I am tricking Angel. But it's *for her own good.*

9

Tackling Angel

At 8 a.m. Wednesday morning Eric was standing in Robert Sparrow's studio, starting bravely on the second paragraph of what had turned out to be an awfully involved explanation of the request he had just made. Robert Sparrow, garbed in an awning-striped terrycloth bathrobe, with his hair on end, was peering at him over a mug of coffee and listening intently.

The artist went on peering for a moment, without speaking or moving, after Eric had finished. Then he blinked, took a sip of coffee, and said, "Sure."

For Eric, the morning became radiant. "You mean —just like that?" he gasped. "You will?"

"I don't see why not," said the artist. "But then I'm not too bright this time of day. Let me see if I've got it straight. One: yesterday evening you set up a tentative deal with your friend at the Hobbyhorse Shop to obtain one wind-up beetle. Two: this treasure— when you get it—you will swap to me for a portrait drawing, as per *our* deal when last we met. However— three: you wish this drawing to be of somebody other than yourself—to wit and i.e., a brand new character in our drama with the unlikely name of Angel . . . or is that bit just one of my early-morning wanderings from reality?"

"No, that's her name," said Eric, who was having to listen pretty intently himself to follow his own story through all this fancy language. "Angel Anthony. I think it's really 'Angeline'."

"Yeah, something always spoils things," said Robert Sparrow. He drank the rest of his coffee and let the mug dangle from his forefinger. "In any case—no problem. I'll draw you a portrait of whoever you like in exchange for your beetle. Whomever. But I have a counter-proposal. To propose."

Eric, who had been about to overwhelm him with thanks, instead said, "Oh," and eyed him warily.

"It's only about the job," said the artist, reverting to his ordinary way of speaking, to Eric's relief. "The one I mentioned to you Monday."

"Oh, the *job!* Oh, sure!" said Eric, hastily trying to imagine what an artist might want him to do. Wash out brushes? Clean cupboards? Sweep the studio? "I could come Saturday afternoons. Or Sundays."

"That'll do. I want you to pose for me. For working sketches. Action stuff, like those." He nodded toward the wall with all the drawings of children running, leaping, climbing, hanging by their knees.

"*Me?*" said Eric, his jaw dropping.

The artist nodded and explained. "My stuff gets lifeless when I work from snapshots. Some people can —I can't. I'd rather make sketches of real live kids— even if I throw away a hundred to get three or four I like." As Eric remained speechless and open-mouthed, he added solemnly, "I work real fast. I don't keep you hanging by your knees for more than an hour at a stretch. And you don't have to learn to fly."

Eric recovered from his surprise enough to grin, though he was still trying to grasp what seemed some sort of baffling joke. "But . . . Why *me?*"

"Why not?"

"Well, I mean—I don't exactly *look* like much. I mean, nothing special. Just like any kid."

"But that's the kind I like to draw—not the pretty ones, not the oddballs—just your generic kid." The artist smiled. "Though that doesn't mean you're nothing special. I like the way you move around—and turn your head. Can't really explain it. But you'll make a good model—that's why Cholly sent you. He's got a sharp eye."

"Well—*sure,* then." Eric was beginning to feel excited, and a little special after all. "I'll come whenever you say. You don't need to pay me, though," he added in some embarrassment.

"Oh, yes I do. It's hard work, holding still—and in uncomfortable positions. But I can only pay minimum wage. And it would only be a couple of hours a week—not every week."

"Oh, that's okay! I—I think it would be fun."

"In that case, how about this Saturday afternoon? Say, two o'clock?"

"See you then!" Eric promised gladly. In fact, he added to himself as he took off on his belated way to school, I'll see you a good while before then—I hope, I hope.

Wednesday, lunch period. By 12:15 Eric was standing in Mr. Lee's little shop, puffing after the four-block run from school, anxiously watching Mr. Lee's face as he mulled over the latest proposal in the long haggle for the Between the Acts box.

"Full resoling job, hm?" murmured Mr. Lee, drumming his blunt, dye-stained fingers on the furrowed wood of his counter.

"*Plus* the price of the materials in cash," Eric reminded him. He added hastily, "Unless it's more than . . . how much do the materials cost?"

"Depends what you want. Now, leather—that comes high. But I got a pretty good buy on some new stuff—wears like iron. Course it's a little stiff at first . . ."

"Oh, I'm sure it'd be fine!"

"Well, then, say—eight bucks cash. And the box."

"It's a deal!" exclaimed Eric. "I'll let you know. Tomorrow."

"Good enough. Shake."

Mr. Lee thrust out his hand and Eric surrendered his own. It was like shaking hands with a nutmeg grater. In another minute he was hurrying back to school, devouring his sandwich on the way.

Wednesday, 3:35 p.m. Eric was dawdling at the Lake Street light, waiting for Angel to catch up. He dawdled until the big bank clock up the street said 3:45 and it was beginning to rain. There was no doorway near to retreat into. He put up his hood and went on dawdling until Melinda Jones came by with two other girls, all under one umbrella and all giggling at him for standing there in the rain. By that time he didn't care.

"Have you seen Angel?" he yelled as they passed.

This produced another burst of giggling of exactly

the type he considered most stupid. It also produced information. Most unwelcome.

"She had a dentist appointment! Her mother came after her at two o'clock!"

So that was that for today. He had to be at Jimmy's in five more minutes anyhow. He dashed across Lake Street on the amber, ran all the way home, and went straight to the Nicholsons' apartment before going upstairs. He found he needn't have hurried. Mrs. Nicholson's boss at Jill's Fabric Shop had phoned, asking her to trade days with somebody who wanted to be off tomorrow.

"But I want you today anyhow," she added quickly. "So it'll give you *two* days' pay instead of one—and me a chance to go over to Lakeview Square at last to get Jimmy some jeans and me some decent panty hose and . . . you *can* come tomorrow too, can't you? I told Jill I was sure you—"

"Oh, yeah, sure," Eric found himself saying automatically. "That'll be okay, you go right ahead . . ."

"It'll be a little later tomorrow—say, four, o'clock."

"Okay."

It was only after she'd left, and the thing was settled, that he asked himself desperately *how* he could sit with Jimmy tomorrow, even starting at four o'clock, when he'd missed Angel this afternoon and hadn't yet talked to Cholly and there was still so much to do? And he couldn't get the kitten when he'd promised— the real action couldn't start Thursday, now. Friday— the absolute last minute—would have to do.

At least, after school on Thursday, he caught Angel without any trouble. In fact, she caught him, before he was halfway to the corner.

"Eric! Guess what!" she yelled when she still was pounding recklessly down the school steps to the street. "I get to go to Disneyland next summer! With Debbie and her mom and dad and little brother! Debbie's mom called my mom last night and asked her, and they talked all about it, and then Mom talked to Daddy and—"

Eric let her tell him the whole story several times, slipping in congratulations whenever she paused long enough. They'd almost reached Rose Lane by the time she finally ran down. He allowed a pause of about two steps, then said casually, "Oh, hey, I talked to that artist, Robert Sparrow, about the portrait for your mother's birthday."

Angel whirled to face him, stopping dead on the sidewalk. "You *did*? Already? I thought you said Saturday! Why didn't you *tell* me? Whad'he say, whad'he say? Is he going to do it? For fifteen dollars instead of twenty?"

"Uh—no," said Eric. "He says he can't make a special price. But—"

He paused again, partly for effect and partly because he wasn't quite sure what he was going to say next. So much depended on precisely how he put it.

"But *what*?" demanded Angel.

"But—um, he sort of owes me a favor. I mean, not a *favor* exactly. I have something he wants. Or rather, I don't have it yet, but I can get it, provided I work out something else first, and—"

"Eric Greene, what are you *talking* about?"

Eric took a long breath and faced her. "It'd take a lot too long to explain," he told her firmly. "And you wouldn't care anyhow. Just take my word for it—I can organize your portrait-drawing for you—I'm almost sure—if you'll make a bargain with me first."

Angel was beginning to look suspicious. "What kind of bargain?"

"Just a—regulation bargain. He'll trade me the portrait of you if I get him the something he wants. Only—before I can get that, you have to give *me* something. Two somethings."

"More than fifteen dollars?"

"No, less. Eight dollars." Eric swallowed. "And your Between the Acts box."

Angel's eyes and mouth opened simultaneously in disbelief. Then she exploded. "Eric Greene, if I've told you once I've told you a million times . . .! Is that all you were doing, just trying one more way to get that box? Well it won't work and I think you're *mean* to make me think I could get a nice p-portrait drawing instead of an old s-school picture and all the time you were just—"

Eric had expected the explosion but not the catch in the voice and the more-than-hint of tears underneath the angry screeching. "Angel, wait a minute," he said, dismayed. "Angel. Hey, Angel, listen! I'm not trying to fool you, honest. I *can* get the portrait. I—Angel, *listen*!"

Angel broke off with a gulp and stood silent, her eyes still brimming, her lower lip turned almost inside out, and her whole square little body expressing total outrage. However, she *was* listening—for a moment. Eric seized it.

"I promise to get you the portrait. No joke. *If* you'll do your share. It's—it's complicated. The box just happens to be part of the deal, and I can't help it, I—"

"You said your friend didn't even want it anymore. You said he could get one somewhere else. You said they were *common*. You said he said—"

"Yes, but he'll take yours if I can get it—and if I *can* get it, then he'll . . ." Eric abandoned his explanations in midsentence. "Look. Do you want that portrait or not?"

After a long, stubborn silence Angel said, "Yes."

"Well, it costs eight dollars to get it—*and the box*." There was another lengthy silence, while Angel scowled past his shoulder at a tree. Eric could feel the struggle going on between her new die-hard determination to have the portrait and her old built-in reluctance to give ground. He waited till he felt the portrait gaining a very slight edge. Then he added, "I'll throw in that antique Chinese lacquer jewel box to take its place."

Angel's eyes returned quickly to his face, her lip turned right side out again and her expression became alert. "Really? That red one with the mysterious gold design?"

Eric nodded, not without a last inner struggle of his own. But for Angel the deal was struck, the decision made.

"Okay," she said briskly. "Give it here. I'll put my cocktail picks in it right now." She held out a hand, fumbling in her jacket pocket with the other one.

"I don't have it right now," said Eric, repressing a strong desire to whoop and yell. He felt as though he had just made it to the top of Mount Everest with no equipment at all. "I told you—I have to work all the other stuff out. You'll have to wait."

"But I don't wanna wait!" Angel protested. "Wait till when?"

"Tomorrow," Eric told her, crossing his fingers—for luck, this time—and sending up a silent prayer. "Tomorrow afternoon around four. If everything goes just right."

"It will, won't it?" Angel was now pushing for the deal as hard as she'd been dragging her feet before. "It better go right!" she warned him. "You promised! You said 'no joke'! You said—"

"I know what I said and I'll do what I said—but I can't *absolutely guarantee* anything until I've done it!" Eric took a long breath. "Meet me on this corner about four tomorrow—and bring eight dollars and the box. So long, I've got to go!"

Eric hurried on toward Cholly's basement, fingers still tightly crossed. So far, so good, he was thinking. And it was pretty far and pretty good. One last deal, and the whole precarious preliminary structure would be complete—or, like the house of cards it reminded him of, it would all come tumbling down.

10

D-Day

Friday lasted about a week. That is, the part before the last bell rang. School *crawled*. The hours *oozed*, like the slowest snail that ever lived. Then finally the bell rang at 3:15, and the day sprouted wings.

Eric snatched things from his locker and was out of the building before the echoes died away, hiding from Angel, watching for Debbie Clark. Luck was with him— Debbie came out alone, hugging her books to her middle and dawdling down the broad steps from the door as if she had all the time there was. Eric didn't. He waylaid her at the bottom and said, "Can I get that kitten now? *Right away?*"

"Oh, yeah! Sure!" exclaimed Debbie, coming to life. "Come on, my mom's over there with the car."

A car! It would save a quarter-hour at least, maybe more. "She won't mind?" Eric said. "Your mom?"

"When you're taking a *kitten?* No! Come on."

They tumbled into the car, Eric in the back seat, muttering how-do-you-do and thanks-for-taking-me and other polite things to Debbie's mother as she drove carefully—and much more slowly than he was traveling inside—to Marina Drive and into the garage. Then they tumbled out again and Debbie led the way down the narrow walkway and into the utility room. Snowflake was on her way across the linoleum, cautiously stalking a fluff of lint. Eric scooped her up without ceremony, dropping his Language Arts book into his jacket pocket.

"I'm taking that wooden ring toy of hers too, you know," he reminded Debbie anxiously.

"Yeah, sure, that's fine. Here it is. How're you going to carry her?" Debbie asked.

"What? Oh." Eric disengaged a needle-sharp claw from his thumb, took the ring with its cord, and reflected belatedly that he ought to have a basket or something. "I'll just—carry her," he said firmly, glad he had left his ring binder in his locker. She'll be okay."

"Okay," said Debbie, whose problem it wasn't. She opened the door. " 'Bye, Snowflake, honeybun, you darling little itsy-bitsy . . ."

Eric escaped, and ran full speed up the little walk to the street, then around the long curve of Marina Drive toward Rivershore. He learned very quickly that Snowflake did not care for running, which jounced her. She squirmed and dug her ten little needles into his hands and uttered surprisingly loud though high-pitched wails of protest. "It's okay, just relax," Eric panted, tightening his grip and trying to run with his knees bent so there wouldn't be so much up-and-down motion. That didn't work. He tried holding her out away from his body to keep *her* smooth even when he wasn't. She gave piercing shrieks and clawed frantically to get back to him, peering down over the side of his hand in terror, then straight at him with big eyes and little pink mouth both wide open. He stopped and hugged her a minute, puffing and wondering exasperately how to work it out, and finally removed the book from his jacket pocket and put her there instead. It was a big pocket, with a flap that buttoned. She trod around in the bottom of it for a moment, silent except for one rather querulous mew, then apparently accepted life as she found it. Eric cupped a steadying hand around her on the outside of the pocket, and went on at a fast, giant-step walk. By the time he passed the bank on Lake Street the big clock on its outside corner said 3:28.

By 3:30 he was in Mrs. Panek's shop, beginning breathlessly on his proposition, which required a good bit of foundation-laying and careful reminding and question-asking. Mrs. Panek was leaning on the counter with a mystified expression, her bare forearms crossed before her like a couple of bowling pins, giving him careful answers.

"Yes, I remember telling you to watch out for 'em," she was saying. "Yes, we still got 'em all over the place, but they don't do a mite of good as long as the varmits keep stealing my . . . The what? What little hook-thing? . . . Oh, that. Why, honey, that's just an old buttonhook, been around here forever, I think it used to belong to . . . no, not specially. But what would you want with that old thing? Folks don't button their shoes any more that I ever . . . Yes, I do use it for that, comes in handy. No, not for anything else I guess, leastways I can't think of . . ."

"Mrs. Panek," Eric said earnestly, "I can solve all your problems. And I'll do it—for that buttonhook."

This produced Mrs. Panek's sudden, and always

unexpected, bark of laughter. "All my problems? My land, honey, you don't know what you're taking on!"

"Well—well, I mean the problems we've been talking about. The mice. And the window shade."

"The *mice*?" Mrs. Panek's gaze sharpened. "Now, how're you gonna do that?"

Eric unbuttoned his pocket and triumphantly drew forth Snowflake.

"My *land*!" shrieked Mrs. Panek. She took one unbelieving look at Snowflake and simply doubled up with laughter. But when Eric set the kitten on the counter her big hand reached out to curl around it. Snowflake crouched away at first, then poked a minute pink nose forward to investigate the nearest finger, and finally sat down and began energetically to wash her front.

"She's a girl," Eric said, all business. "She won't prowl around like the toms do. She likes to chase things. She'll be company for Frank. She'll grow fast and then she'll hunt your mice. Mice don't hang around places where people keep a cat."

Mrs. Panek wiped her eyes with a corner of her handkerchief and recovered from her hilarity, though she was still shaken by occasional little subterranean chuckles. "This cat looks more like a dandelion clock than a dangerous hunter," she said.

"The mice won't think so," Eric promised.

"Maybe not. Though so far"—another irrepressible quiver shook her—"she's not much bigger than they are." Eric kept anxiously silent, relying on Snowflake to do his sales job from this point on. She had finished tidying her front fur and was starting on her left leg, sticking it straight up into the air in a businesslike way and going to work as if somebody were holding a stopwatch on her. "Makes herself right at home, don't she?" said Mrs. Panek, watching. "She sure is cute, though. Pretty fur! Y'know, they say you can tell a good cat by the quality of its fur. This'n feels just like velvet. Or eiderdown or somethin'." The big hand was moving gently down Snowflake's shoulder—just one finger stroking the fur. Mrs. Panek looked at Eric, her eyes still brimming with amusement. "You gonna tell me to wait till she grows up, then she'll pull down my window shade for me too?"

"No. I've got something else for that." Eric produced the wooden ring on its cord and put it on the counter.

He thought at first it was going to send Mrs. Panek off again, but she only gurgled, quavered "My *land*," and dragged out her handkerchief to blow her nose, shaking her head. "You're a world-beater. You know that, Eric honey? You're gonna go far. Here, take your buttonhook." She fumbled in the drawer beside her and handed it over. "This little white fluff-ball might never catch a mouse in her life, but I can't resist her. Or you neither. Haven't had a laugh like that in thirty years."

"Oh, *thanks*, Mrs. Panek!" gasped Eric. "Thanks a *lot*! I really do appr—Oh, I forgot, here's something for Frank, too. A kind of bonus. Will you give 'em to him? I've got to hurry!"

He dug in his jeans pocket for the two Indian Head pennies Maggie had given him Saturday, deposited them on the counter beside the preoccupied kitten, and with a last grateful pat on Snowflake's white fur, was on his way.

It was now 3:42.

At 3:47, flustered by a sixty-second delay at the light on Lake Street at Cedar, he arrived at the Hobby-horse Shop in Long Alley and fairly burst in the door, causing its glass to rattle and the little bell to tinkle frantically. Then he longed to slink right out again, or vanish into thin air or something, because there were customers in the shop—three middle-aged ladies with big sensible-looking purses—and all of them, along with Maggie, had turned to stare at the cause of all the noise.

"Sorry," said Eric in a voice barely louder than a whisper.

"Anything the matter, Eric?" Maggie asked calmly.

"Oh, no, I—I just—"

"Be with you in a minute, then. Hang around." Maggie turned back to the ladies, pointing to something behind them so they'd look away from Eric, and went on telling them whatever he'd interrupted. He stood on one foot and then the other, hurrying inside. A clock on the nearest old table said 4:15, giving him a terrible shock until he realized it wasn't running. By 4:31 he had to be on the bus. He fidgeted over to the glass case and located the beetle. Still there, ready and waiting. He reached into his little inside jacket pocket and took out Dad's daguerreotypes of the stern-looking people who weren't related to him and held them in his hand with Mrs. Panek's buttonhook. He was ready and wait-ing, too. Now if Maggie could only . . . He cast a longing look her way and found her walking quickly toward him. The ladies huddled together in the background, peering at something on the far wall.

"What's up, Doc?" said Maggie. "Come for your beetle, have you?"

"Yeah!" Eric breathed, and came back to anxious life. He held out his offerings. "Are these okay?"

"Oh, more than okay!" Maggie exclaimed as she took them. "Downright jim-dandy! That's an *ivory* handle on your buttonhook, I do believe . . . No, early celluloid. Great either way. So now you want the wind-up, right? I love your Great-Great-Grandpa or whoever he is," she added as she walked around to unlock the case, still admiring the daguerreotype.

"No relation," Eric told her happily. And then he had the beetle in his hand and couldn't stop the grin that spread all over his face. Everything was working out—every single thing—so far. "Thanks a lot! I'll be back after a while—and I'll be in an *awful* hurry by that time," he said urgently.

"I'll drop everything," Maggie assured him as she relocked the case.

She went back to her customers, and Eric went out the door. It was 3:55 exactly. He'd told Angel to meet him at her corner at "about" four o'clock. He was going to be late.

Because of slowpoke traffic lights and a sudden maddening stream of cars coming up First Street from Rivershore, he spent six minutes getting across to Diamond and another three racing along it to the Garden Shop yard and Robert Sparrow's outside stairs. He took them two at a time, feeling his legs go achy and then limp, so that he staggered across the balcony at the top and nearly fell through the open doorway.

"Jumping Je . . . Oh, it's you, is it?" Robert Sparrow came to meet him, bristly blond eyebrows high, bringing an aura of painty smells. He was holding a brush and wearing an ancient bib apron liberally smeared with color. "Walk right in, always welcome—no need to bust the door down." He followed this with his abrupt grin, so Eric merely grinned back and concentrated on letting his breath catch up with him, wordlessly holding out the beetle.

The artist stuck the brush behind his ear, took the beetle, and looked it over with delight.

"Great!" he exclaimed. "Simply great! Right up there in a class with my rabbit and my old tin butterfly. And now you want a piece of paper that solemnly swears, in so many words . . ." He was moving sideways to his drawing board, nodding as he talked, along with Eric, who was nodding because he hadn't yet enough breath to answer questions. "Okay. I do solemnly swear—" He picked up a pencil and tore a scrap off a block of tracing paper with the same hand, still holding the beetle in the other. "—do solemnly swear," he muttered as he wrote. "Portrait of one child, female persuasion, name of Angel . . . time to be arranged . . . mutual consent—I like 'mutual consent,' don't you?" he said to Eric. "Got a nice legal ring to it . . . Fee paid and acknowledged, signed, R. Sparrow, Esq.—That's to impress her, that 'Esq.'" he explained to Eric. His pencil scrawled the signature, then swiftly sketched in the little sparrow underneath. He folded the paper one-handed, thumped the crease in and gave it to Eric with a flourish. "There you are—all signed and slapped. On your way now, I want to play with my beetle."

"Wow, thanks!" Eric puffed, slipping the paper into his pocket after one admiring glance. "Thanks a *lot*. I'll see you Saturday!"

"Two o'clock!" said Robert Sparrow, busy winding the beetle. Eric, glancing back as he went out the door, saw him stoop down to send his new toy scuttling across the floor.

There wasn't a clock to look at. Eric, heading back along Third at a restrained jog so as to have some breath left for Angel, figured it might be about 4:11, or maybe 4:12. It couldn't be much later. It just couldn't. And she'd better be there, waiting—he hadn't even one minute to spare.

She was waiting—he saw her as soon as he cut over to Rose Lane and started toward the Market Street corner a block away. Obviously she'd arrived on time; she was now sitting grumpily beneath a tree, projecting indignation and boredom like laser beams. She scrambled to her feet as she spotted Eric, her mouth already opening to begin with, "Where you *been*?" and go right on from there for maybe half an hour that he didn't have to waste.

"Sorry," he yelled, forestalling her. "I *said* 'about four.' That's what it is." He arrived, puffing, digging into his pocket. "Here's the paper. Here's the Chinese box. Gimme the other one, I'm in a hurry."

"You must be!" Angel said, staring at him as she accepted box and paper and reached into her own pocket to feel around. Then she reached into another pocket and felt there.

"Come *on*," Eric begged. "Haven't you *got* it?"

"Yes, yes, yes, it's here somewhere, don't be so—

here it is. You'll have to wait while I take all my cocktail picks out of it and put them into the—"

"Okay but hurry *up*!" Eric, jogging in place in an agony of impatience, heard the chimes on the Episcopal church strike the quarter-hour. "Angel, hurry!"

"Well, you're making me so nervous—! There, *take* it, for heaven's sake!" Angel thrust the Between the Acts box at him and squinted down at her paper.

"The money! The money! The eight dollars, remember?"

"Oh, yeah. Just a second. I put it—no I didn't, I think I—here it is. Five dollars. Plus another is six, and one is seven. And twenty-five, fifty, sixty, sixty-five—" She finally made it to eight dollars, counting five last pennies into Eric's tense hand. Then her attention returned to her paper. "Now, how do I do about this portrait thing? When am I supposed to—"

Eric was already on his way. "That's up to you!" he yelled over his shoulder as he sprinted back toward Lake Street. Only two more calls . . . no, three. But at least they were fairly close together. First Mr. Lee— and he'd soon be halfway there—then only four blocks, short ones, across to Cholly's . . . well, call it four-and-a half . . .

A red-headed young man familiar from somewhere —Riverside Drug? Quiggly's Hardware?—was just leaving Mr. Lee's shop with his package under his arm as Eric shoved breathlessly in. They exchanged uncertain greetings—Eric's also unintelligible—then he was gone and Eric was half-falling onto the counter and triumphantly slapping the Between the Acts box down in front of Mr. Lee.

"Well, by gosh you finally got it for me!" Mr. Lee picked up the box to inspect it. "It's a dilly, too! Revenue stamp and all . . . Say, boy, you've been running too fast! Better have a drink of water and siddown a minute. Come on back here, and I'll—"

"Can't," Eric panted. "Big hurry. Can I have that —paper?"

"Oh yeah. Time for that there promissory note—" Mr. Lee reached a stained, blunt-fingered hand toward his stack of work tags and found a pencil stub in the sagging pocket of his brown apron. Two bold black checks, one on each half, then he tore the tag on its perforation and handed the customer's half to Eric. "There y'are. That there ticket and eight dollars—"

"I've got the eight dollars now." Eric undid his clenched hand and Angel's money, down to the last five pennies, dropped onto the counter in crumpled wads and little clinks. "Thanks a lot, Mr. Lee—gotta go now." He heaved himself off the counter, caught sight of Mr. Lee's watch, and shot out the door without remembering to say goodbye. The watch had said 4:21.

He was at Cholly's by 4:24—and a half, according to Cholly's old clock, which, old or not, was usually right. Eric flung himself on the daybed, forgetting its concrete-like solidity, and gasped "Ouch!" before he could stop himself.

"Yep, it's a sturdy one, that one is," said Cholly, rotating off his work stool and reaching for his teakettle with the same motion. "Chap I bought it off of garnteed them springs for twenty years, and it musta lasted thirty by now. What *you* need, son, is a cuppa. You're all wore out."

"No, Cholly—thanks—no time. Look. Remember

yesterday? Our deal? The resoling job?" Eric hauled himself upright and handed the ticket over. "There 'tis. Mr. Lee said so. That's all you need."

"No joke?" Cholly scratched his shaggy whiskers as he grinned from the tag to Eric. "And he'll gimme a whole resole job on these old boots?" He stuck out a foot and considered it. "Can't honestly say it's before time, can I?" He chuckled richly and stretched an arm up to the shelf above his worktable. "Here 'yar, then. I emptied it out ready last evenin'. And my best to Maggie."

With an unsteady hand, almost reverently, Eric accepted Cholly's stoneware kerosene bottle that had once, long ago, held ginger beer and would fetch thirty dollars in Maggie's shop. It was a moment too rare for thanks. He transferred the bottle with tender care to his jacket pocket, then thrust out the hand again. Cholly enveloped it in a hard-calloused grasp, squeezed painfully, then let go. Eric took off for the street.

He was scarcely aware of running now. Maybe I've got my second wind, he thought. But it wasn't like that, it was as if he had suddenly learned to fly, like the girl in Robert Sparrow's drawing. He wanted to skip and hop and turn somersaults—something inside him was lighter than air and simply trying to rise. It was only his hundred-odd pounds of flesh and bone that kept him touching earth at all.

He was crossing First Avenue for the sixth time that day when the sight of a bus rumbling around the corner from Rivershore brought him down with a shock that jolted like Charlie's daybed. It couldn't be 4:30 . . . no, that bus was 40, which went southwest—not Number 37. Even so. Heart thumping from more than speed now, Eric raced the final block and a half, glancing fearfully far up Lake Street for the first dreaded flash of yellow that would be Number 37 easing around the curve from Evergreen Drive. When he plunged into Long Alley it had still not appeared. The glass shop door shuddered and Maggie's "OPEN" sign swung wildly on its cord as he plunged into the shop.

There was nobody there except Maggie, whose voice he heard operatically shaking the rafters from the rear-most room. He yelled, "Maggie! Maggie!" and it broke off, changing to a non-operatic shriek: "Eric? Is it D-hour? Coming, coming, I'm on my way!"

He hurried across the room, crying, "I've got it! I've got the ginger beer bottle! Look, it's just the one you wanted, now can I have the eighteen dollars, and can you hurry please, because my bus—"

"Fifteen dollars," Maggie panted, hurrying just as urgently from the other direction. They met in the middle of the second room. "Sorry, I was up on a ladder, took me a minute—"

"Eighteen, wasn't it?" said Eric uneasily, handing her the bottle, which produced her dazzling smile.

"Oh, what a beauty! Oh, what an absolutely—Eric, you're a pal and a half, I'll buy you a double-dip Baskin-Robbins whenever you say so, come on to the cash register, I'll give you fifteen smackers this minute, and—"

She whooshed past Eric, who stared after her, wide-eyed. She'd said it *twice* now. So was it her mistake, or had *he* got it wrong in the first place, or—"Maggie!" he quavered, running to catch up. "Maggie—*eighteen* dollars, didn't you tell me? Don't you mean eighteen dollars?—Please?"

Maggie halted and peered down at him. "No, fifteen's what I told you—*if* I was sure beforehand my customer'd take it for at least twenty-five. Got to make a living—I told you that too, remember? *You* told *me* you needed eighteen."

Though nineteen would be better—that was what he'd said. Eric did remember. His heartbeat ran down like an old, tired clock.

Maggie added, "I assumed you'd find the last four bucks some other way."

"Yeah," whispered Eric. He did have the nineteenth dollar, the bus fare, put aside from the extra Jimmy-pay; it was in his jeans pocket right now. But after all he wouldn't be needing it. As he stood trying to get this through his head, trying to comprehend disaster, a distant familiar rumble made a faint chiming among the glass shelves in the case, and sent him dashing in panic to the door. He was just in time to see the Number 37 go by the foot of Long Alley, heading for Rivershore and the city. "It's *gone!*" he wailed. "I've *missed* it! It's too late, the whole thing's over, today was my last chance and I blew it, but I tried so hard and I ran so fast and—"

"Eric!" Maggie was beside him, gripping his shoulders, bright blue eyes staring into his face. "Eric, hush up and look at me. *Please* tell me what this is all about."

Eric swallowed his despair—he had to keep swallowing—and told her in a few bare sentences about Jimmy and the boots and all his swaps. "But it didn't work," he finished. "It just didn't. There wasn't quite enough time."

Maggie let go his shoulders and slowly straightened, her lips pursed, her gaze still absently on his face. Her thoughts, he could tell, had gone somewhere else. "Stand right there," she said suddenly. "Don't move a muscle. I've got to make a phone call."

"It's too late," he said. He was so tired all at once that he had to sit down on the edge of one of the roped-across chairs. "Today's the last time I can go to town, and the bus is gone, and the sale ends tomorrow."

"There's another bus, pal." Maggie was striding toward the back room and the phone, still carrying the ginger beer bottle. "Number thirty-nine stops up there by the Safeway at four forty-five . . ."

Eric didn't hear the rest, if there was any, because she shut the door. He sat on his chair-edge, gradually tensing up again, wondering wildly if a bus at 4:45 would make it to town before the stores closed, and whether it might be 4:45 already, and who Maggie was talking to on the phone, and what kind of miracle she was trying to pull for him. Before he could wonder anything else she flung open the door and came striding back, looking at her watch and talking fast.

"Okay, we're all set. Mrs. Thing—I shouldn't call her that, nice lady, it's Mrs. MacGillicuddy or something—says she'll definitely take the bottle and what's more I soaked her thirty bucks. So I'm giving you eighteen of 'em right now—" There was a jingling *crash* as the cash register drawer flew open. "—and one more as commission, and you've got two minutes to get to Safeway and you *phone* me tonight to tell me how it all comes out . . ."

Eric was already out the door, jamming the money in his pocket, yelling back something over his shoulder, and crossing his fingers again as he ran. They were going to grow that way pretty soon, what with one thing and another. He kept them crossed—except while paying his bus fare—all the long, rumbling, pokey, endless way into town. He tumbled out at last and took to his own flying feet again for the two-block sprint to the shoe store.

He got there seconds after the doors closed. The tall, handsome young black woman was still turning away inside, the bunch of keys in her hand, plainly visible through the glass. Eric flung himself against the door and knocked frantically with both fists, shouting, "Wait! Wait! Please wait, I've got to buy something!"

The woman glanced back, frowning, peered in a puzzled way at Eric, and as he redoubled his knocking and pleading, came back and unlocked the door. She opened it two inches and said, "Store's closed, babe. Gotta come back tomorrow."

"I *can't* come back tomorrow! Oh, please, it'll only take a minute. I want that pair of cowboy boots you showed me once and I've got the money right here, all ready—see?" Eric dragged the crumpled bills out of his pocket and thrust them at the two-inch opening, right up under the black woman's nose. "It's awful important! At least—I mean . . ." A horrible thought hit Eric. "You've still got them, haven't you? They haven't been sold?"

The woman flapped a languid hand at Eric, shaking her beautiful head in a way that made her earrings swing and glimmer. "Now, how you expect me . . . *Which* cowboy boots? We got cowboy boots coming outa our ears around here. You better calm down, babe, you gonna bust something."

"Well, couldn't I just come in a *second*—"

"Okay, okay, come on, don't have a hissy." The door opened six more inches. Eric was inside like an eel. It closed behind him, and the lock clunked into place with a jangling of keys and bracelets. "Now you gonna have to tell me—"

"They're red and black, one hundred percent vinyl, on sale for seventeen ninety-nine, whatever size is six and three-quarters inches long, or maybe seven—"

"Oh, yeah. Seven inches long—now I remember. It all come back to me." To Eric's astonishment she threw back her head and laughed a long, rich, bubbling laugh, meanwhile heading for the stockroom. "Yeah, we still got 'em. I kinda hid 'em behind some others that day. I figured you be back."

Thirty minutes later Eric was jolting homeward on the 6:10 Number 37, hopelessly late for dinner, hugging a box of red-and-black cowboy boots in a death grip against his chest.

11

The View from the Top

It was Saturday morning, and life was back to normal. That is, as normal as you could call it when you felt ten times happier than usual, and ten times luckier, and maybe fourteen times more pleased with yourself than you ever had before. It was normal in that Eric was sitting in Jimmy's living room instead of sprinting full-tilt here and there or *planning* to sprint here and there, or only half-listening to Jimmy's excited chatter because of solving multiple jigsaw swapping puzzles in his head.

Today the chatter was twice as excited as usual, and Eric was listening wholly and with contentment. There was only one subject under discussion—the red-and-black one hundred percent vinyl cowboy boots, which were on Jimmy's feet and fit perfectly, and were everything either of them had hoped for. Fifteen swaps, it had taken—no, *sixteen*, counting that curtain-ring— but the end was worth it.

The surprise, too, had been exactly as Eric had visualized it—with only one disconcerting note: the reaction of Jimmy's mother when the box was opened. She had gaped at the boots, then at Eric, then had made all sorts of intensely embarrassing faces in her efforts not to cry while trying to *take the boots away from Jimmy* and put them back in the box. "No, Eric, you *mustn't!* Your own money!" she kept saying.

Eric had stared at her aghast, then leaped to the rescue, wrestling the right boot out of her hand as politely as possible—Jimmy had already recaptured the left—and begging her just to *look* at Jimmy. She had looked, and let the other boot go, and said nothing more, though she hugged Eric hard enough to make him grunt before she left wordlessly for work.

Eric, who was still looking, with great enjoyment, reflected that if he ever decided to collect anything, it was going to be expressions like the one on Jimmy's face. But they'd be hard to come by. Rarer than even the rarest of old English ginger beer bottles.

"Hey, Eric!" Jimmy had hauled one stick-thin little leg across the other knee and was peering delightedly at a boot. "Those designs are *stitched* in there! Not just drawn, they're stitched! See that star? Wow, isn't that something? These'll last *forever!*"

"They won't fit you forever," Eric couldn't help reminding him. "You going to cut the toes out when they get too short?"

"Aah, no!" Jimmy gave an ebullient giggle. "I'll paste 'em in my memory book! Or frame 'em and hang 'em on the wall!"

Eric laughed with him. Everything seemed worth a laugh today. He wasn't even sure it was Jimmy's expression that was making him feel so extra good—so free and light and midsummery, like floating on his back in the lake. That was part of it, but not all. He'd liked the whole boot operation—the swapping, and thinking it up himself, and getting to know people like Maggie and Robert Sparrow, and making complicated deals. He might do more of that; Maggie had told him when he phoned last night that she'd give him five percent commission on whatever he brought in that she could sell for more than five dollars. And he had his new job posing for Robert Sparrow, plus the old job too. He was going to make pretty good money—too bad there weren't any boots to use it for now.

There was Christmas, still ages away. Naturally he always got Dad a present, and Willy. But it was beginning to seem a shame to use real money for anything, when you could accomplish so much with swaps. Idly, he thought again of what Dad had said that day. Maybe Robert Sparrow would swap an hour's posing for one of the drawings he didn't want—the ones he said he threw away . . . Eric was sure Dad would rather have a drawing of him hanging by his knees or flying over the treetops than any dumb school picture. And that wouldn't take money either.

Well, he'd save his money. He'd *save up to buy a bike*.

Of course! thought Eric, electrified. Why didn't I think of that first thing? I don't need a *new* bike. I could make a deal with Willy—that whenever he gets that twelve-speed I get his old ten—for a down payment and something or other per month. Maybe even swap him stuff for the something per month. I'll have to find out things he wants.

"Or else," Jimmy was saying hopefully, "I might get a bigger pair when I outgrow these. I might go on getting bigger and bigger pairs till I'm all grown up, and by then I'll be a regular cowboy and I'll need a horse! I might be able to ride a horse someday—don't you think so, Eric?"

"I don't really know," Eric told him, wishing he hadn't heard the slight wistful note in Jimmy's voice. A tiny cloud of worry appeared in his mind's clear sky. He said uneasily, "Are you *really* set on being a cowboy when you grow up?"

Jimmy gave one of his teasing giggles, and Eric knew it was a joke on him. "No! I'm set on being a nuclear physicist, silly. How could I be a cowboy with these dumb legs? What're you gonna be? Oh, I know. A librarian."

Eric hesitated. "Yeah, well, maybe."

"That's what you always said."

"I know," Eric admitted. "But lately . . . well, I've been doing some thinking."

A *lot* of thinking, he reflected, along with all the swapping and sprinting around. And a lot of discovering things about Eric Greene, most of them new and surprising. Even the thinking was new and surprising—because it wasn't a bit like Dad's. He seemed to have swapped that, too, for a set of ideas all his own.

Which made it swap number seventeen.

"So you *aren't* going to be a librarian?" persisted Jimmy.

"Oh, sure, I might," Eric told him. He smiled and slid further into his chair. "But I dunno," he added comfortably. "I just might go into business for myself."